Pay You in Hay

WILLIAM J. HENRY, M.D.

To Dr. Nagle,
Hope you enjoy
my father's stories.
Thanks for everything.
Laura Henry
Grimstad

FIRST EDITION

 RED APPLE
PUBLISHING
Peggy Meyer, publisher
15010 113th St. KPN
Gig Harbor, WA 98329-5014

Printed by Gorham Printing
Rochester, WA 98579

ISBN 1-880222-32-9

Library of Congress Catalog Card Number 99-74597

Cover design by Amy McCroskey

Cover photo by Ann Henry

PREFACE

My HUSBAND, DR. WILLIAM HENRY, started writing episodes of this book shortly after he retired. He did not sit down and write the book all at once but would write his thoughts about different people and different events that happened during his thirty years of practicing medicine in the Methow Valley in Washington state from 1960 to 1990.

He was devoted to the practice of medicine and especially enjoyed responding to emergencies. It was not unusual for him to accompany the ambulance crew when they responded to calls. He loved teaching and training EMTs (Emergency Medical Technicians).

In retirement, Dr. Henry missed taking care of people and would have continued to do so if his health had permitted him. Writing about his experiences was great therapy for him. His family and some friends suggested he put these thoughts into book form. He wrote with fond memories of the people involved. However, the names of the patients have been changed to protect their privacy, although many of them are now dead.

Dr. Henry spent about a year revising and rewriting before he was satisfied with what he had written. He had had such an interesting practice that he had to choose carefully the episodes he wanted to share. He did complete the book before he died and was looking for a publisher. I knew how much it meant to him to have it published, so I searched for about a year and finally found the right one.

Dr. Henry liked to tell a good story, and *these are good stories*. He thoroughly enjoyed reliving his experiences as he was writing this book. I hope you will get as much enjoyment reading them as he did writing them.

On February 22, 1998, Dr. Henry died. Aero Methow Rescue Service is a reminder to everyone that he wanted to bring the best medical care to the valley. Daughter Cindy, as head of the service, continues that tradition.

—Ann Henry

ACKNOWLEDGMENTS

Special thanks to those who encouraged Dr. Henry in his writing. Among those are Jan Hoem, who did extensive proofreading and made excellent suggestions in the beginning, and Jim Goodsell, who spent many hours with the final proofreading. Also thanks to Bill Shafer, Joe Zemites, and Erik Thompson who gave him continuing support.

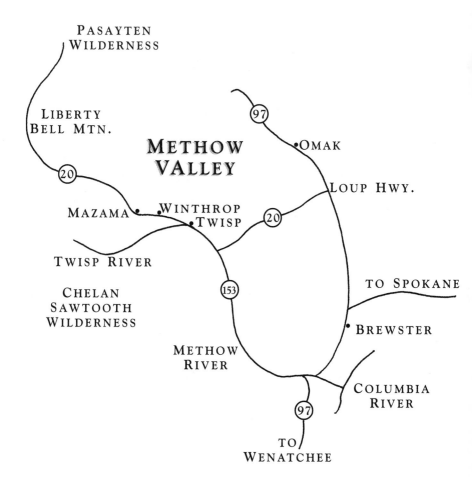

TABLE OF CONTENTS

Chapter 1

In the Beginning

FOR AS LONG AS I CAN REMEMBER, it was taken for granted in my family that I would become a doctor. I have no idea who made that decision or just when it was made. Somehow, in my family's value system, being a doctor was the pinnacle of success and the noblest of callings.

For a time I wanted to be a driver of fire trucks, but that dream faded. For a while I thought I would be a forester. That ambition died. I even thought that someday I would go west and search for gold or silver, a fantasy fanned by the Depression that plagued us in the 1930s. But two goals outlasted all the others, and these two had the added advantage of my family's approval. I wanted some day to own a car, and I wanted to go to medical school and be like Dr. Danny.

Some of my earliest memories are of Dr. Danny O'Connell. He made house calls when I was sick or injured. He came to our house one day to repair my lacerated forehead. I remember my father taking me to his office in downtown Jeannette, Pennsylvania. I remember my mother and her sisters extolling his great virtues as a man and as a *doctor.*

During the Great Depression my father was making about $150 a month—but he *did* have a job. I'm not sure that Dr. Danny was always paid, but when my parents called, he came.

My aunt married a doctor. I remember little about my uncle as he was in those days. But I do remember that when he came to court my aunt, who was living with us, he always paid a little attention to me.

I entered grade school in 1934, predestined to be a doctor. Soon afterward I lost touch with my role model, Dr. Danny, because my family moved from Jeannette to Pittsburgh. There my father, with a master's degree in education, was making about $200 a month. In the big city we didn't have a family doctor like Dr. Danny, and we missed him.

I went on through grade school and eventually through high school. When well-meaning persons asked what I was going to be when I grew up, I always said I would be a doctor. That meant someone who delivered babies and took care of kids with earaches. They didn't tell me about typhoid fever, tuberculosis, syphilis, diphtheria, and tetanus. That's what doctors took care of in the 30s—and for those challenges there was no sure cure. This was before the advent of antibiotics. For the doctor it was a life of sorrow and defeat and frustration. No one told me that real doctors cried some nights when they went to bed.

All of my family's efforts were centered on getting me into a good college, and then it was up to me to make grades good enough to be admitted to medical school. Right after college I was admitted to the University of Pittsburgh Medical School.

I don't intend this narrative to be an autobiography, so I will be brief about the next ten years that took me through medical school, internship, and the Naval School of Aviation Medicine. Five years on active duty in the Navy were challenging, and in many ways those years prepared me for my career as a backwoods country doctor. In the Navy I did search and rescue in the Aleutians, trained crews for high-tech special weapons delivery, and supported my pilots as they qualified on the decks of aircraft carriers. The Navy took good care of me and promoted me in advance of schedule. I liked the Navy because I was good at what I did. I fitted into my picture of what a Naval Flight Surgeon was and did. But there was no assurance that this pleasant state of job satisfaction would continue. Every three years the Bureau of Naval Personnel moved us. With the achievement of rank, there was no assurance that I could continue being a flight deck flight surgeon who flew Naval aircraft.

What I wanted was to be a country doctor. An event that happened on 13 December 1957 gave me my first real taste of what country doctoring could be like.

I want to remind you that I grew up in a big industrial city, Pittsburgh. When the Navy sent me to Kodiak, Alaska, I found myself involved with search and rescue in the Aleutian Island chain. On that day in 1957 I responded aboard a rescue amphibian-type airplane to a call for help from the Aleut village of Perryville on the south shore of the Alaskan Peninsula bordering the North Pacific Ocean.

Perryville was notable for what it did not have—no reliable water supply—no sanitary sewage disposal—no trees. Its all-Aleut population had been moved there from an outer Aleutian island by the U. S. Navy during World

War II when the Japanese were threatening the Aleutians (and did occupy Kiska and Attu). The United States government had dropped the Aleuts at Perryville and said, "This is your new home." They built houses out of driftwood and roofed them with bits of dimension lumber that washed up on the shore as flotsam. The rainfall in that part of the world is about 100 inches a year, which did not make for a pleasant environment.

The village was managed by an Aleut chief, whose name now escapes me. He was intelligent and could read and write. With what the U.S. Government gave him, he did a good job managing his village. Their food and supplies came from the ocean and the Sears Roebuck catalog. The mail boat visited once every three weeks.

The week before my being called, a young Aleut had visited Anchorage. There he developed a case of measles and brought it back with him. Now nearly everyone in the village had measles. The native populations of the world are frightfully susceptible to the white man's diseases such as measles, smallpox, tuberculosis, and even the common cold. They have lived an isolated existence and have never had the opportunity to develop natural immunities.

Two children at Perryville were dead. Others were coughing and febrile. My senior medical officer in Kodiak said, "I know you have no cure but go and see if you can prevent or treat some of the pneumonias that are killing these people."

Our Navy amphibian landed in the bay. The pilot had to keep the aircraft constantly in motion because spray from the propellers was freezing on the control surfaces. The village chief sent a whale boat out to get my medical corpsman and me.

I was a bit thrilled by the experience. I sat up in the bow of the boat panning the area with my new motion picture camera. When I got nearer to the shore, I realized that the men of the town were down to the shore to meet me. They were filming ME with THEIR cameras.

My corpsman and I visited every house in the village. We found the two girls who had died of this disease, both about twelve years old laid out on their families' dining room tables. They were draped in white and surrounded by candles.

We could do nothing there, but elsewhere there was pneumonia, draining ears, rashes, fevers, vomiting, and diarrhea. Every house presented some type of medical challenge.

The chief went with us with his notebook. He took down specific medication orders for each child and adult, but soon I ran out of medicine and could give only aspirin.

It was a profoundly moving experience. In Pittsburgh I had never witnessed such a display of disease. As the hours passed, my pilot became very impatient to leave the village. The village chief asked me to stay, but I had to decline his request. (In the future I carried my own personal overnight kit with food and water should such an invitation ever come again.) I left with a ton of guilt on my shoulders but knowing that I had used every pill, shot, and medication that I had. If I had stayed, there was nothing more I could have done for those poor people.

As soon as we were airborne, I got on the radio and called Coast Guard Radio Kodiak and explained the situation to their operations officer. I told him that at least twenty-six of Perryville's children and adults needed to be hospitalized. Late the next day a Coast Guard cutter reached Perryville and did indeed evacuate most of those sick people to the Alaskan Native Service Hospital in Anchorage. The doctors and nurses at the ANS hospital were very busy with their desperately ill new patients—but there were no more deaths.

About two years later, after I became a country doctor in Twisp, a new pastor moved to town to supervise one of the churches. He and his wife had adopted an "Eskimo" child from Alaska. When I saw the child, I told the family that she was not an Eskimo. I could tell the difference after three years in the Aleutians. This little girl was an Aleut, and she remembered when a Navy doctor came to her village and gave her a shot of penicillin. I was profoundly moved.

I had learned that to be an effective country doctor (in Alaska we call them bush doctors) you must go to where the sick people are. You, doctor, will not make much money. You, doctor, will have a soul overflowing with the memory of grateful people and an intense personal satisfaction that transcends other paths your medical career might have followed.

It was with a background of experiences like Perryville that I eventually came to Twisp to be a country doctor.

Chapter 2

What Do
Country Doctors Do?

TWISP IS A TOWN OF 800 PEOPLE in the eastern foothills of the Washington Cascade Mountains. It was supported by logging, a lumber mill, cattle, alfalfa, and a vast potential for recreational wilderness endeavors. The town was cared for by an older doctor who was approaching his own retirement. The nearest hospital was forty-two miles to the south.

The distance to the hospital didn't deter me at all. For three of my years in the U.S. Navy, I was in charge of medical aspects of search and rescue in the Aleutian Island chain that separates the Bering Sea from the North Pacific Ocean. There were no hospitals in that world, and I got along quite well.

My arrival in Twisp was a turning point in my life. I fantasized that on my day of arrival the people of the town and surrounding valley would welcome me with great celebration and enthusiasm. When I arrived, hardly anyone noticed. I lived on the main street of the town (which was four blocks long). I walked to work in the morning and then home again for lunch.

I extracted a little bit of money from the care of the sick to cover my personal expenses. I found that rural folks think that doctors have lots of money. We were therefore paid last, if at all. For the first year in my idealized country setting, my family and I lived on about $400 a month (1960 dollars). At the end of the first month, I had to borrow $3,000 from the bank to keep going. At the end of the second month, the note was expanded to add another $1,000. A compassionate banker, who became a life-long friend, wanted a young doctor in his town and was prepared to pay the price. At the end of the third month, I began to pay back the loan.

My wife, Ann, who was accustomed to an active U.S. Navy social life, was lonely. I worked about twelve hours a day. We had three children with a fourth enroute. No one stopped off at the house to see how she was adjusting. There were no welcoming parties or visits. She spent a lot of time alone or with the kids.

I was up at 6:00 each day, drove forty miles to the hospital to make rounds and then forty miles back to Twisp to see my office patients at 9:00 a.m.

Because Ann wanted to meet some people, she started a kindergarten in Twisp—in the girls' bedroom. Gradually she was noticed by the other women in town, especially when she started picking apples at harvest time. Doctors' wives are different. They don't usually do things like that. Fortunately, Ann's commitment to the out-of-doors, which included skiing and hiking, kept her and our daughters occupied. There was a small ski area about twenty minutes from town. Ann started a ski school, which occupied her weekends for about fifteen years. If you are expecting welcome-aboard parties or invitations to afternoon bridge, you're not cut out to be the wife of a country doctor. The details of my family's early adjustments to Twisp are also not the subject of this work. The subject is what I did, and did not do, as a country doctor. At first, people view you with suspicion. Some say you are too young. Older men will not be spontaneous about their personal problems in talking to a much younger male. When they do come to see you, they will be badly hurt or very sick. Both the men and the women of the Methow Valley had a preconceived idea of what a doctor does. When they want you, you must be ready to yield to their expectations of you. (Those of us who accepted this challenge were also frightened. We were aware of what we did NOT know, and they were not.)

Soon after my arrival, when my new office was still full of unopened packing boxes, I was greeted by a knock at the door of my home. Ann and I were entertaining two other physicians who were also new in their respective small towns. The alarm at the door was occasioned by one of the old-timers in town who was "snake bit." He was in a sweat, holding a significantly swollen left hand. He did indeed have a rattlesnake bite. The three physicians at the Henry house took him to my new office and proceeded to care for him. I busied myself with trying to calm the victim. Dr. Bratrude was in a back room reading a printout that described how to reconstitute snake bite antivenom. Dr. Cowan was in another room reading the small print about how and where to administer the antivenom. Mr. Flint was on the examining table in the front room completely ignoring me because he was certain that this was his last day on earth. We did administer the antidote. We didn't do it correctly but Mr. Flint was immediately relieved because he had received the *shot*. He was my first hospital admission and later became a very good friend.

Since then I have taken care of about twenty rattlesnake bite victims. I now do it correctly and travel about our state giving lectures to other physicians on how the problem must be managed. They don't teach you that in medical school. Since I graduated from the University of Pittsburgh and Drs. Bratrude and Cowan were from Chicago, snake bites are not a problem in those cities. It is a problem in Twisp. Mr. Flint went off to the hospital (where they had never heard of Dr. Henry). The three doctors retired to the Henry house to water down their own unnatural high.

We still talk about how ignorant we were in 1960. Remember, though, that there is stupidity and there is ignorance. Ignorance is curable. If you don't know, you can find out. That is part of those long years of training that you endured. You must never communicate to the patient your opinion of your own inadequacy. Call it "fake factor" if you must.

There are certain principles that apply to all emergencies and challenges. Follow those principles and *primum non nocere*. This Latin phrase, well known to doctors, means "above all, do no harm." You must be honest with your patients. Don't try to do anything with, or to, these people that you know may hurt them. You must do your own personal debriefing after challenges such as this. When you face the enormity of the task that you have voluntarily accepted, you will become frightened. Remember, it was your own choice to become a country doctor. Not many at faculty level in our medical schools have any idea about the enormity of the isolated rural challenges.

Country doctors take care of people. Sometimes you find that you are caring for someone who would prefer not to be under your care. You make friends with him or her. You can sense the patient's reticence to be friendly to a young doctor just out of his training. Yet the patients kept coming.

They expect you to see them in their homes. You must come when they call. I had to leave the weddings of two of my daughters to care for one person who was injured and another who thought he had had a stroke. You go. You respond to "call backs" to your office after supper. Two or three times a week you get out of bed between midnight and 6:00 a.m. to go to a farmhouse for someone who is worried or frightened.

You work weekends because the valley where you are the only doctor has become a recreation center for Puget Sound people. In Seattle the folks are used to round-the-clock emergency departments in the hospitals and urgent care centers. They expect the same service in Twisp— *and they get it.* They don't know that you are the only doctor and you don't tell them. The Henry family didn't take vacations because there would be no one there when your patients are hurting or injured. You take a bit of time on Wednesday afternoon to go for a walk in the hills behind the house (provided you are not in bed trying to catch up on lost sleep).

There was a day when I was closing the medical center in the late afternoon. Our car was packed and Ann and the five children were already loaded in the car. This was to be our first vacation in about six years. A mother approached me in the midst of this scene with her daughter who had sustained an injury to her wrist. I apologized and declined to see her. I explained the details of our airplane schedules and motel reservations. Reluctantly she went elsewhere—a drive for her of about forty miles each way. Over the next twenty-five years, she and her family never came back to me for medical care.

There are always surprises. A logger was using his chain saw to cut the close-in limbs off the tree before he felled it. This entailed operating the chain saw above his head and in front of his face. When operating a chain saw, there is always the danger of a kickback wherein the saw bounces off the log or tree and comes back onto and into the operator. The kickback is unpredictable. Some loggers install anti-kickback devices on their saws. Some do not. Such was the case for Mr. Reed.

The saw kicked back into his face. The blade split his face, opening the skin over the forehead, the nose, both lips and in the process destroyed a few teeth. It was a nice vertical cut that allowed me to see into his face where the center of his nose used to be. Both eyes were all right but the central incisors, both upper and lower, were gone.

A chain saw does not cut like a knife. It takes out a kerf of tissue the width of the blade—about a quarter of an inch wide. They never taught me about chain saw injuries at the University of Pittsburgh School of Medicine. This was horrible. The weather was bad. It was snowing. I retired to my personal office to think about this one. My nurse set up for the repair and was horrified that I was considering sending the victim over 100 miles for the services of a plastic surgeon. She informed me in direct language that I was the surgeon and if I wanted to build a reputation in this neighborhood, I would have to fix this man's face.

Actually it was quite simple. Several times I asked out loud if there was perhaps another surgeon in town—a question to which I already knew the answer. A surgeon will anesthetize a face by blocking six nerves with a local anesthetic. This is what I did and Mr. Reed became comfortable. From that point on, it was a layered closure of the wound. We all know how to do this, but I had never attempted it in so sensitive a place. I found some pieces of cartilage and bone lying loose in the wound. With those pieces I rebuilt his nose. The teeth I could do nothing about, but if he had brought them in with him, I would have replaced them in their empty sockets.

Repairing the lips required that we carefully align the vermilion border of the lips and then, using tiny sutures, gradually pull the skin over to close the defect. When I was through, he had a pretty good looking face, albeit a bit narrower in the vertical plane. Mr. Reed could see and he could breathe. His oral hygiene was not too good in the first place, so this gave him an opportunity to have a set of dentures constructed at the expense of the workmen's compensation program of the state.

The operation had required about two hours' work in the emergency trauma center that occupied part of my medical center. When we were finished, my nurse and I congratulated ourselves, took the obligatory Polaroid picture, and discharged the patient. He refused to go to a hospital. Instead, he drove back to the logging area to retrieve his chain saw. He felt that if he had been hospitalized, someone would steal his saw and that would make his boss very angry. Mr. Reed did not come back in the required forty-eight hours for me to evaluate his wound. He didn't want to take off from work. He <u>did</u> return in seven days for suture removal. He did this only because he had an appointment with a dentist that day.

I now see Mr. Reed on the streets of Twisp. It is twenty years later and we are both retired. When I get close to him, I think I can see a scar. His nose looks pretty good for one that was reconstructed out of torn pieces of cartilage and bone. I am pretty proud of that job. It was my first big one.

It was merely the process of anesthesia, local cleansing, and performing layered closure just as we were taught in medical school—but on the face, never! Mr. Reed is amazed that I am impressed. He thought all doctors knew how to do repairs such as this. They do not.

What else did I do? I rescued people in the mountains and the wilderness that surrounds us. To do this I organized an ambulance company of about twelve people. The skills and techniques of the emergency medical technician had not yet been defined. We created our own rules and protocols. We bought a Chevrolet Suburban, supplied it, equipped it, staffed it, and made it into an ambulance. Much of what we placed in the ambulance we scrounged, modified, or just simply made ourselves. That homemade ambulance served us for twenty-six years.

I gave lectures in the school system, trained emergency medical technicians, sat on the school board, went to church, and occasionally said hello to my family. Sir William Osler claimed that the practice of medicine was "a jealous mistress who demanded all and was never satisfied." I had read that in medical school but never knew what Sir William meant. One day I found that I had, indeed, created that jealous mistress for myself. The practice demanded all. She is an expensive mistress. She gets fed first. Periodically I realized that this was what I wanted, trained for and worked for. By then I had a mountain of debt on my back, owned an expensive medical building, and had built a small empire that allowed me the satisfaction of being a country doctor. I found that I had to work hard to feed this demanding mistress who now led me like a pet on a short leash. This was what I thought I wanted. No, it WAS what I wanted. The price was severe. No one told me the price. Yet I stayed.

I liked the people. I'd like to tell you something about these folks. The intensity of a doctor's involvement with a grateful patient cannot be described. There is great satisfaction in seeing the person you "fixed up" back at work again and back with his or her family. There are the lives you saved. There are the babies you delivered coming back to you and asking you to deliver their babies.

There is satisfaction in the versatility you are developing. You are becoming a master in many of the medical trades. This is balanced by the humble feeling that maybe you shouldn't be doing this—but who else can do it? Who else will do it? There are always the big city specialists, but those doctors are 100 or more miles away. You are the best there is for these people. By accepting the challenge, you become better at it.

The country doctor learns to take his own x-ray films, to troubleshoot the equipment, and to make a competent reading of the films. He sets up and runs his own laboratory and teaches nurses and aides to do simple, but important, blood tests. When the country doctor sees that things are not right, he comes up with a solution that is not in the books. He becomes an expert in trauma and emergency medicine. He does what he has to do, and by doing it, he becomes better at it.

Chapter 3

My First House Call

MY FIRST HOUSE CALL WAS TO THE RITCHIE HOUSE up the Chewach River valley.

Bette was of the real West. She lived during the gold rush days of the Chancellor and Baron gold fields in the upper Methow Valley. She did not earn her living by digging gold. She earned what she had by entertaining miners and making moonshine. She served moonshine, chicken dinners, and herself for a price.

Later in her career she found it more lucrative to hire other women to do what she did best. In this way she became one of the successful madams of our gold digging days. As a part of this life style it was important that Bette also drank a bit of her own sauce.

It is now 1960; the gold digging days are over. Several of the girls are still in town. One is still working at her profession. Bette is married to Sid, a merchant seaman who is home occasionally. Sid is an alcoholic and spends most of his time at home, drunk.

At sea Sid knew every naughty house on the Pacific rim. He knew where to hide his booze aboard ship and, in general, was a violent, impulsive individual who couldn't be trusted. He contributed nothing to the marriage. Neither did Bette. She wasn't the best of cooks, she was frequently drunk, but in bed she performed to the highest expectations of Sid Ritchie.

I had been in my new practice about five days when a call came to me from Sid that Bette was having coughing fits. He demanded that I come to see her. It was not an easy set of directions that he gave for the trip to their home. But I did find my way. I drove into their yard and heard the continuous spasms of coughing that he had described. I also noticed smoke coming from the living room.

In an overstuffed chair in that living room sat Bette wracked by fits of coughing. She was very drunk. On a bed at the back of the living room lay Sid in his underwear, unshaved, and unwashed. He also was so drunk that he couldn't get out of bed. "She's over there, Doc. Give her a shot and make her shut up."

I approached the chair in which Bette was sitting. It was immediately apparent to me that Bette was coughing because the chair was on fire. With little help from Bette and no help from Sid, I moved her to another chair. Then I was faced with the task of getting that chair out of the house. It was smoking heavily and was too wide to fit through the door. It had to be turned on its side and dragged, pushed, and coaxed through the narrow door. There was no water available. I dragged the chair far enough from the house that when it burst into flames it would not do much damage. Five years later the skeleton of that chair still occupied a prominent place in the Ritchie yard.

Bette survived the ordeal but had no memory of my

assistance. Sid took another swig from the Mason jar that held his moonshine. For me, there was nothing to do but to go home. Before I did, I carried seven or eight pieces of wood into the house and stoked the fire in the stove. It was going to be a cold night, and neither of them was in any condition to make the trip to the wood pile. I sent the Ritchies a bill for $7.50 (to include mileage). The account was never paid.

There are a lot of Bette Ritchie stories in the valley. Sid contributed his share of them, but he was usually in Osaka or Bangkok. Sid eventually developed cancer of the throat. When we discovered it, it was not operable. He couldn't swallow food or water. My surgeon friends created a feeding tube that entered the small intestine through the abdominal wall just beyond the stomach. It was through this tube that Sid was to introduce water and liquid food preparations. This he did and maintained some semblance of life.

He did notice that the feeding substance didn't always clear the tube and would remain in the tube until the next feeding. This worried him. He proceeded to clear his feeding tube with four or five ounces of whiskey after each feeding. This was quite ingenious and simplified his nutritional and metabolic needs. It did require over a fifth of whiskey a day to keep the feeding tube clear. It was in this state that he went to sleep one day, a sleep from which he never awakened.

Bette lived alone when Sid was at sea. There was a morning in the spring when she slept late. She got out of bed to go to the bathroom, tripped, fell, and hurt her hip. Actually, the hip was broken. She could not get back into bed. She was now in her early 70s but slept in nightgowns that reflected her previous professional behavior. The gown was flimsy and did a poor job of covering her more intimate features. She noticed an electric company lineman who was working on a power pole outside her home. She managed to call to him to come to her assistance. He did.

The problem was to get a mostly unclad ex-prostitute up into bed and restore some heat to her cold body. They tried several approaches but the hip pain was too great. The final approach consisted of the workman straddling her torso, putting his arms under her arm pits and lifting her up onto the bed. What he did not know was that before Bette had called him, she had telephoned the doctor to come also. He was in this position, trying to lift Bette onto the bed when the doctor walked into the room. The doctor, who had known Bette for many years, cleared his throat. The itinerant workman placed her back on the floor, said "Oh, shit!", picked up his tools, and walked away.

Bette had her hip pinned. Several years later she fell and fractured the other hip. Before she would permit me to place her in an ambulance, she called one of her rum runners to the home. This was a boy in his late teens, who, for a price, delivered alcoholic beverages to a list of customers that Bette maintained. They paid dearly for the privilege of being on her distribution list. She gave explicit directions as to who should get what and how much money she expected in return. When her rum runner had his instructions, Bette permitted me to put her in the ambulance. (That ambulance was before the days of the Chevrolet Suburban ambulance that we created. It actually was the back of a panel truck that the town of Twisp used for its water-line maintenance.)

Bette survived the pinning of her hip and was soon

back in business. She continued to be an interesting person. She never listened when I talked but did demand my full attention when *she* talked. Gradually the Bette Ritchie stories came at less frequent intervals. One morning we visited her in her trailer at the trailer court. Some time in the preceding days she had gone to bed and never awakened. The cause of death was listed as *natural* for an interesting lady who had seen a lot of life.

Chapter 4

Three Women at Home

I LIKE PEOPLE. Seeing them in their homes is sometimes a duty for a physician, sometimes a privilege. When people come to us, we tend to see them at their best and as they want us to see them. When we see them in their own homes, we see them as they are in a natural environment. We see how they live, what they eat, what they drink, how neat (or not neat) they are.

People are pleased to have the doctor visit them in their homes. They are usually very relaxed and proud that their doctor took the time to come and see them. Inevitably the telephone will ring when I am in their homes. The conversation usually includes the following phrase: "I'll call you back. The *doctor* is here now!"

No age group is unique in its appreciation of the house call—the mother with the sick child, the family with an aged parent, a group of elderly friends trying to do it all themselves. All deserve attention. So seldom do doctors give this attention. House calls take a lot of time and some doctors just don't have that luxury. The practice of medicine is not an academic pursuit. It is a series of humanistic involvements.

I had in my practice a group of three women who lived together. Although they were dependent upon each other, one assumed a place of primacy. There was never a formal election. A *pecking order* seems to be a natural phenomenon when two or three are gathered together for mutual support. Each member knew her position and defended it. There was no concept of superiority or inferiority in status, and yet one did rise as the final decision-maker.

Such a one was Edna. Edna was a retired nurse who had at one time operated a nursing home in her home. When the state became more rigid and severe in its licensing protocols, Edna's nursing home license was not renewed. It is not that she did not give good care or had a bad home. She simply wasn't an institution in the eyes of the State Department of Health. Two of Edna's guests elected to stay on with her as live-in friends. She was still the *first lady* and owned the home. They paid her what they could, and among them they lived a very comfortable existence.

My first house call to this home was to see Sammye. Sammye was a chronically ill member and the sickest of the three. When I approached the house, I found it to be a sturdy structure on a bluff overlooking the river. It was well landscaped. A large car sat in the carport beside a big inboard-outboard motor boat. There was an entry foyer. I stepped down three steps into a sunken living room quite tastefully furnished and decorated. Two walls of the living room were glass windows giving a dramatic view of the river valley below them. The other two walls consisted of bookshelves containing one of the best personal libraries I

31

had seen in the valley. The books were standard classics and represented an interest in classical antiquities.

Three of the shelves contained long-play-records of all the usual classical works of the masters. In addition there was a music section with records of the big bands from the 40s. The floor was attractively carpeted and was always swept and clean. In the library section of the room was a pool table complete with all the usual equipment and supplies to permit a healthy round of *eight ball* and its variations. Behind the pool table was a small bar stocked with a good selection of spirits.

Three women made their home here. Edna owned the house. She was a pleasant, square-built woman with an air of authority. She took her responsibility toward the other two seriously and took very good care of them when they were sick.

Mary was the oldest. She was always dressed well. She was pleasant and acted as if she had just come home from church. Mary had silver hair, regularly trimmed and waved by her hairdresser. She was a delight to chat with and spoke of a long interesting life. Mary just didn't want to be a bother to anyone. One weekend her irregular heart sent a small blood clot, which we call an embolus, to her left arm. Improperly treated it would cost her the arm. But Mary, not wanting to be a bother, put off until Monday to tell me about it. Fortunately, time had not run out, and my surgeon friends were able to remove the clot and save her arm. This concerned me that another clot would go to a more serious part of her body and create a stroke. In spite of my best efforts, this is exactly what happened several years later.

Sammye was the sickest. She was the classicist of the

group; she owned all of the books and the music. She was well read, not only in the classical antiquities but in current literature as well. She was always sick, but her illness was under control. Sammye was an ex-alcoholic. She suffered from neuritis of her legs which dated back to her drinking days. At some time in her life, rectal suppositories of belladonna and opium had been prescribed for her. Since she already had an addictive physiology, it is no secret that she became dependent upon her opium suppositories. Sammye was *hooked* on opium. I don't know how she got the suppositories because I never asked. Under certain circumstances this is a legal drug for short periods of use, but for Sammye this period of use exceeded three years.

Yet, she was the intellectual of the group—well read, well informed, and a delight to talk with. We spent many evenings talking about the Trojan Wars, the attack on Rome by Hannibal with his elephants across the Alps, and the works of Benjamin Franklin. At the end of one of these sessions she gave me her copy of POOR RICHARD'S ALMANAC. At another she gave me a copy of Voltaire's CANDIDE, and on another evening her copy of Vergil's GEORGICS. She hated television, so we listened to Beethoven. I remember her as a sick, elderly lady, addicted to opium and classical inquiry.

One night Sammye died. There was no major terminal event. She simply went to bed one night and quietly died in her sleep. Edna found her and called the funeral director. She felt no compulsion to call me or any doctor for confirmation. Edna was in charge of all things, in death as well as in life. (The funeral director quietly yielded to her primacy and called me the next day to request a formal death certificate.) Edna cleaned up the room, made the bed, and put away Sammye's clothes. Then she went back to her own bed to sleep away the rest of the night. The next morning at breakfast, Mary commented about how late Sammye was sleeping. She missed her company at the meal. Edna looked up from what she was doing and said quietly, "Oh yes, I meant to tell you about that. She died last night."

And so their life went on. Later Mary died of a massive stroke. Edna lives on alone, bothered by anemia and a sore back. She is accepting and serene about her role in life. She is satisfied that she did well in her life, and she will always continue to be a pleasant woman and a competent nurse. I liked those ladies. I got to know them in their home. It was a privilege that gave me insights I could never have enjoyed in medical office encounters.

Chapter 5

House Calls

AS I'VE SAID, DOCTORS MAKE HOUSE CALLS. That fact was a part of my training. Much of my early reading, while a grade school student and while in high school, was about doctors and their way of life. From this exposure there was born in me an ideal of how a doctor should be and how he should act. Buried somewhere in that ideal was the commitment that doctors saw their patients in the patient's home.

This did not preclude seeing people in our offices, but home visits were a part of the physician's role. When I built my own practice, I outfitted a housecall bag that was a mirror of a hospital emergency room. From it I could tend to and treat just about everything that might confront me in a person's home. Even during my days in the United States Navy, I was distinguished as a rare physician who would make a house call to see the sick child of one of my sailors.

Physician prejudices against the house call grew rapidly. Some of this new prejudice was dictated by the ever-increasing fear of litigation against the physician for providing less than an ideal standard of care, some because the physician didn't know the geography of his area well enough to get around in it, and some because it took too much time from the physician's "valuable time frame."

I did not fear litigation. Fear of attack to obtain narcotics sometimes entered the equation. I simply didn't carry them. People appreciate the personal attention they receive from their physician. I made friends with my patients by helping them, and friends seldom sue friends. If I could not do what was necessary in the home, I told the patient and suggested another approach. The patients appreciated this and would usually follow my advice.

I did know my territory. You get a map, you ask for some directions, and you meet people. You will find your way around. The time factor was indeed a problem when you live in a rural area. It is a burden to leave an office full of people or to leave your own supper table or your bed to travel twenty or thirty miles to see a minimally sick person who could have waited until the morrow or who could have come to the office earlier.

Many times house calls were worthwhile in terms of human misery. Sometimes they were a response to an egocentric demand of an ungracious person. Often the person requesting the service was unaware of the inconvenience that the request caused me.

During house calls you meet people on their own ground. This can tell you a lot about the patient and help you to understand the cause of his illness and the problems he may have following your instructions. Requests for house calls don't come as often as today's physicians may think. In a period of thirty years I made many house calls, but the majority of them were made to a minority of patients who somehow got the idea that that was how it was supposed to be. Some of the calls were at great inconvenience and difficulty to me personally. Most of them were at night. About half of them were really necessary; the other half were motivated by fear or worry and resulted only in the dispensing of reassurance and support.

Many house calls are imprinted in my memory. One of these was the call I received on New Year's Day from a man who lived on the Rendezvous Road. The road was not plowed for the last mile to his home, so I had to park the car and walk over a snowmobile path to his partially finished home. Upstairs on a mattress on the floor was a thirty-five-year-old man. He had a body temperature of 105, was covered with perspiration, and when he coughed, about every ninety seconds, nothing came up. Each cough, he said, made his head feel larger. His lungs sounded awful. This was influenza. Many people have died of this disease. I understand that now. Die is just what he wanted to do. While I was there, he had to go to the bathroom. This he accomplished by crawling on his hands and knees. There was nothing that I, like the doctors of old, could do. I dispensed some powerful comfort medicine, a large dose of aspirin, and the usual admonition to get lots of bed rest and fluids. Bed rest? He couldn't do anything else. What a dumb thing for me to say! When I got back to my office, I gave myself a booster dose of influenza vaccine. I am a believer!

Some of the most memorable house calls were those I made on Cal Whistler. You have to have known Cal Whistler to have understood my problems. First of all, Cal was a sick man. He was a retired insurance broker from Portland. He and his wife, Alice, had retired to a one-bedroom cabin about twenty-five miles north of my home in Twisp. The area where they chose to retire was in a zone of our valley called Early Winters—with good reason. It was often snowing and cold. The road to Cal's cabin was frequently not plowed open and an over-the-snow approach was often necessary. Cal and Agnes found the use of the bedroom was clumsy, so they moved their beds into the living room to bring them closer to the fireplace, the kitchen and the front door.

Cal suffered from a chronic progressive lung disease called pulmonary emphysema. In this disease a person loses the elastic recoil of his lungs and has to consciously control each breath—in and out. The patient's exercise tolerance is severely reduced and he coughs a lot. Such was the case with Cal. Occasionally Cal would develop a bronchospasm wherein the small air passages in his lungs would go into a spasm and suddenly decrease the amount of air he could force into the air sacs.

If ever there was anyone who needed to be close to medical care, Cal was that person. A common cold had the potential of killing him. He lived in fear that his next breath would be his last. Cal also lived under the fear that although he might die tonight, he just might (with proper medical attention) live forever. To do so meant that he would outlive his money, and this he feared more than dying.

Cal wanted me to believe that he had once had a busy sex life. He was constantly telling me of his many conquests before, during, and after World War I. Stories like this from an aging curmudgeon must be taken for what they are. If they were true, Cal had had an interesting adulthood. If they were not true, they represented Cal's last chance to prove to me that he was not always as I found him. I smiled, listened, and did not take notes. When he died, we found in his personal belongings old photographs of totally undressed women with personal notes to Cal written on the back. Perhaps his stories were true! When I visited him in a nursing home later in his life, I found copies of *Playboy* magazine in bed with him. It seems he never lost interest.

I first met Cal in my office late one night. Cal was seventy-five years old. He was experiencing the first of the attacks of bronchospasm that would haunt him for the rest of his life. The attack was easily treated with a slow intravenous injection of aminophylline. Cal fell in love with me that night. There is nothing more satisfying to a person with lung disease, who thinks he is dying, than to be able to take a full breath and exhale it with ease. Cal asked if I would see him again, here in the office or at his home, should this attack ever recur. I gave my sincere assurance, not knowing where he really lived. That was a piece of reassurance that later cost me many a night's sleep.

It didn't take long for Cal to test my integrity. On a winter day at 2:30 in the afternoon, I was seeing people in my office. There were two in the waiting room and one person in each examination room. The call came in that Cal couldn't breathe. Cal made his own calls because Alice, being a bit deaf, could not use the telephone. To listen to Cal gasping over the telephone was indeed terrifying.

At that time in my life I was driving a British sports car called a TR-4. (Most un-country- doctor-like, I confess, but it was a lot of fun to drive.) I threw an oxygen bottle, an assortment of drugs, syringes, and respiratory assist paraphernalia into the car and started out for Early Winters. It was December, but the roads were bare.

The deer herd for which the upper part of our valley was famous was out in the pastures along both sides of the road. The TR-4 cornered well and held sixty miles an hour on those narrow roads. A deer decided to run along with me. Another one entered the road next to my left front wheel and tried to get in front of me so she could make the traditional contact with my grill and headlights. I was a bit upset over the prospect of having my TR damaged. When I applied the brakes, the car squealed. The deer, hearing the new sound, became frightened and, turning toward the car, jumped over it. She left a few guard hairs where she dragged her feet over the roof. But she fared well and bounced off into the pasture on the other side of the road.

The car was not damaged, and I was now suffering from a surge of adrenaline and excitement. However, I drove on to Cal's cabin a bit more slowly. Fortunately, when I reached the cabin, the road had been plowed free of snow, and I was able to drive up to the door. I collected all of my respiratory gear and burst into the cabin, expecting to see Cal either dead or very blue.

He was neither. He sat in a straight-back chair dressed in an old-fashioned cotton nightgown and tasseled night cap. He wore slippers but no socks. Alice sat quietly in another chair, knitting. There was a fire in the fireplace and the cabin was comfortable. Cal leaned forward, spread his legs so that the nightshirt sagged between his knees to the floor. In his hand he had a stopwatch. Without looking up at me he checked the stopwatch and said, "Twenty-two minutes. That's not bad, Doctor, for twenty-five miles."

Cal was not sick. He just wanted to see if I would really come if he called. I suppressed the natural urges that appear in circumstances such as this. I sat down with him, reviewed the weather, the new cabin and how the winter was treating him.

When I got back to my office, my patients were still waiting for me. Cal, on the other hand, got on the telephone to his daughter and said something like, "You know that doctor I found up here? He makes house calls!"

Over the next fifteen years I saw a lot of Cal. He really liked me. I controlled his lung disease but could do nothing about his progressive cerebral deterioration. Eventually he displayed a full-blown case of Alzheimer's disease, and it was necessary to place him in a nursing home. Before his loss of mental competence, Cal had lent me $8,000 to apply to a new medical center that I was building. The pay-back terms were "interest at seven percent payable monthly and principal of one thousand dollars a year payable on the first of March." On the first day of each March, I made a ritual visit to the nursing home with a check made out for one thousand dollars in Cal's favor. We talked a bit. He told me some more lies about his days of Eros and wine.

The Alzheimer's syndrome progressed, and throughout much of the year he knew no one, remembered nothing and could not carry on a sensible conversation. Yet on the 25th of February every year until he died, I received a telephone call from the nursing home. It was Cal and he was reminding me that we had a date on the first of March and, if it wasn't too much trouble, could I come early. He was concerned that he would not live until the first. I repeatedly said no. I was faithful to the March first visit. When I arrived, he was up, dressed, and shaved. He accepted the check, and we talked and had a nice visit.

When I went in to see him the following week, he looked at me in anger and said something like, "Do I know you?" It was that way all year. I continued to be responsible for his care in the nursing home. Then, predictably, on February 25th the following year, there came the usual telephone call. Cal was lucid five days each year.

Cal continued to deteriorate and quietly died in his sleep one evening. He was ninety-three years old. I had known him for eighteen years. He did, indeed, outlive his money. He had become a part of my way of life, and the memories of his personal foibles and personal integrity live on.

Chapter 6

The Night
the Ambulance Died

ONCE A FAMILY GETS THE MESSAGE that their doctor makes house calls they never forget it. Some are demanding, some apologetic, some humble, and some incredulous. A majority of my house calls have been to a minority of my people. The rest of the world (who don't know that this service can be had) are the incredulous ones. They (usually the father) will call, frequently late at night, and describe a very sick child. Their next question concerns when I can meet them at the medical center to examine the child. I say something like, "If I'm going to go out, why do both of us have to go out? Tell me where you live." This is followed by a pause while the reality of what's going to happen sinks in.

The child I saw that night was a twelve-month-old girl who was very sick with influenza. It was February. The year wasn't important but the season was. It was winter. The mother had been "steaming" the child all day and throughout most of the night. It was one o'clock in the morning. This child could not breathe. Every inspiration was accompanied by retraction signs of the soft tissues of the neck and chest. Physicians consider this an ominous sign that portends respiratory failure. Susan had a temperature of 103°. Mother was concerned, father was concerned, and I was worried. This child had classical influenzal pneumonia.

You must understand there was about twenty inches of snow already on the ground, with more falling at the rate of two inches an hour. The nearest pediatrician and hospital were forty miles to the east over a 4,000 foot mountain pass. I had no respiratory therapy in my town, and it was apparent that this child would need complex airway maintenance and care.

Doctors are supposed to be able to see the future, mainly because they have been there. This child was not going to survive the night—even if Betsy (my nurse) and I stayed in the home and attended to the child constantly. There are some things you just can't do in the home.

I had an ambulance with four-wheel-drive configuration parked at the medical center. While Betsy worked with the baby and the mother, I went back to town to get that ambulance. I assured myself that it was set up for most airway emergencies including intubation of the trachea. I drove it back to the home, and Betsy and the mother got into the front seat with the baby nicely tucked under Betsy's down parka. I called the sheriff's dispatcher and explained what I was doing. This was greeted with an incredulous remark and a question as to whether I had checked the weather and really knew what I was doing. I didn't answer.

As I left town, I noticed a local police car sitting at an

intersection. We blinked lights and waved. He was going home soon at the end of his shift. That policeman was Bill Ervin, one of my emergency medical technicians. He was pleased that it was me and not him who was out that night.

The ambulance sputtered a few strokes and then caught on again and proceeded as fast as that much snow will permit a four-wheel vehicle to proceed safely. I approached the uphill side of the pass that separated me from the hospital. Betsy was assisting the child to breathe with an occasional mouth-to-mouth puff. In between she was using a suction device to clear out the secretions that the child could no longer cough up. Mother sat with her face in her hands. Ten miles out of town the ambulance quit. It was dead. It would not fire, and we were presented with the odor of raw gasoline coming from the engine compartment. It was very quiet. I heard the snow hitting the roof of the ambulance. I heard the labored breathing of the baby. I could hear the sobs of the mother.

I remembered Bill Ervin sitting in his police car back at the town's main intersection. I still had a battery, so I activated my radio and asked if he was still on the air. The reply was, "Yes, can I be of any help?"

A collective sigh went out over that emergency channel. I asked him to pick up my other ambulance and bring it out to the ten-mile post on the Loup highway. It was not a four-wheeled vehicle, but it was big and had dual rear tires.

It really wasn't very long, but it seemed like an eternity, before I saw the flashing red lights as Billy delivered the ambulance to me on that cold road. He had it heated up, the oxygen on, and the suction supplies all laid out for us. We transferred the baby and nurse and mother and continued on to the hospital. It was not a comfortable trip. The baby continued to deteriorate, and I drove with a careful compromise between the desire to get to the hospital and yet to stay out of the ditch and to stay on all wheels. It was the longest trip of my life.

At the hospital the pediatrician and his intensive care staff met us. Susan was taken into the intensive care unit. The doctor obtained the necessary blood samples, x-rays were taken, and life monitoring equipment was installed on the child. The pediatrician and the respiratory therapist managed to get a small tube into the trachea to assist in breathing. The respiratory therapist attached a respirator to the tube to ease the tremendous effort of breathing that the child was experiencing. Inserting that tube was not an easy job, but it saved the child's life. The nurses were able to remove the secretions from the airway with their tiny suction tubes. Overhead heat lamps were turned on to restore the body heat the child had lost during the trip across the mountain pass. The child would not suck. One of the nurses inserted a feeding tube through the mouth into the stomach for insertion of food. The pediatrician allowed a measured amount of fluid to enter through his intravenous access line.

With constant around-the clock-attendance, the child survived. It was two weeks before Susan could go home. Her mother stayed with her constantly. Betsy and I went home by another route that avoided climbing the 4,000 foot pass. It was almost sun-up by the time we arrived back in Twisp.

Meanwhile, back on the Loup highway, ten miles from town, Bill Ervin was standing there scratching his head wondering how he was going to get home. A tow truck solved the problem. The gas line was reconnected, and the ambulance, which we call Rescue Blue, still runs on snowy nights.

Susan was a child whom I had delivered in my office about twelve months earlier on a cold winter night. It had been snowing that night. In about eight months we had another office delivery for this family. This time it was not snowing, but the weather was cold. Shortly thereafter the father, quite prudently, moved his family to Southern California. To this day no one will believe the story of that family's first three years.

* * *

Harvey Samson was a kindly old gentleman who came into this valley shortly after the turn of the century arriving by covered wagon.

One night he fell and struck his head on a sharp object. The result was a four-inch laceration of the scalp. I saw him in his own bedroom. I just couldn't make Harvey get dressed, go out in the cold, and travel the mile to the medical center. The wound had to be closed surgically. I went back to the emergency room and collected every conceivable instrument and suture material and bandages. I went back to Harvey's bedroom, anesthetized the skin around the wound and surgically closed it. A week later I removed the sutures. Harvey was a pleasant gentleman with a great memory. I sat in his living room for a long time while he told me about life in the early 1900s. He was gracious and appreciative for the bedroom surgery. It did not surprise him. He felt that that's what doctors do. In his life experiences, he was right. That's what country doctors did for him as he was growing up. Why change?

Chapter 7

Heart Attacks

IF YOU HAVE BEEN READING MY STORIES with a critical eye, you will notice that my life in Twisp seems to be full of drama, excitement, life and death. It isn't always so.

In 1960 I thought I knew it all. That's the reason I took on the challenge such as this. I had been to Alaska, the Smoky Mountains, the Algonquin Provincial Park, and I had been to sea. What other challenges could the good Lord have for me? I had passed the important tests and always came out with a good score. In general I knew what to do!

I remember it was a weekend. It was in the winter about 8:30 at night. Rancher Sam Stevenson asked me to drop by and have a look at his wife. Sam and Sal operated a large cattle ranch. They did it all themselves. Their kids had grown and had gone off to college or started their own families. They were in their late 40s. These two did the baling, brought in the bales, stacked them, and fed them back to the cows and calves during the winter. There was no one else. A ranch like this does not make much money. They couldn't afford the usual hired hand, especially in the winter.

Sal was on the couch. Sam had to help her into the house after she had moved the evening lines of irrigation pipes in the hay field. She wore a pink nightgown—out of style for a tough farm wife. She was smiling but she was hurting. She held a clenched fist over the mid-part of her chest. When doctors see this, our minds always go first to *heart attack!* Her pulse was weak and fast; her blood pressure was low. There was a bit of sweat over her face and forehead. You didn't have to be a second-year medical student to recognize the clinical appearance of a heart attack.

Although city doctors may not understand it, I did have in the back of my car a portable electrocardiograph. I hooked up the wires, and the machine showed that one chamber of Sal's heart was not functioning as it should. She was indeed having a heart attack.

"Sal, you are having a heart attack! I think you should go to the hospital."

"I can't do that, Doctor. Who would get Sam his breakfast?"

"Well, you see, Sal, when people get to the stage you're in, the heart can suddenly stop and there is no more!"

"So, what do you do about it when that happens?"

(Remember, this was 1960. We had not yet defined the advanced cardiac life support protocols. Hospitals did not have defibrillators. There were no cardiac intensive care wards. We didn't know how to use cardioactive medications.)

I said: "We call in the family."

"Fine," she said. "I'll take my chances. Can you come by every evening and see how I'm doing? I happen to think you are wrong with your crazy diagnosis. I'm not having a heart attack!"

I gave her an injection of morphine and gave her husband a vial of nitroglycerine pills and showed him how to give them to her when she hurt *real bad*. I also left my telephone numbers and cursed him with eternal hell fire if he should ever let his driveway clog up with snow. The ambulance might need to get to the front door in a hurry.

For the next week, I drove by the ranch every night after work. One day Sal was up and dressed and setting the table for Sam's supper. "It doesn't hurt any more. I don't see any reason for you to come by!" I dropped the frequency of my house calls to Monday and Thursday and soon stopped them altogether. Before summer was over, she was driving the swather to cut the hay and that fall she was helping Sam bring in the hay.

I felt guilty that I had not insisted on her going to the hospital. But the hospital was forty miles away and her ranch was only six miles from my home. Maybe it was better this way. Nowadays we are seldom so lucky. If I had permitted this to happen in the1990s, the legal system that we work under would have been severe with me, and we might have gone to court if some of the more frequent cardiac complications had occurred.

Last year, at a senior citizens potluck dinner, I met Sal. She told all her friends how great I was because I took care of her *heart attack* at her home thirty years ago.

Now I must tell you the other side of the story.

Doug Phelps was a good friend. He had a higher opinion of his own decisions than he did of my recommendations. Doug was about fifty-five years old. He experienced crushing chest pain that radiated to his jaw and left arm on the slightest physical provocation. This pain was relieved by a nitroglycerine tablet under his tongue.

"Doug, you have heart disease. It's progressive. There will come a time when we can do nothing for you. Now we can. It involves an operation to direct new blood to the portions of the heart that are starving for blood. Want to talk about it?"

"Nothing doing, Doc. You guys are always trying to find some new way of getting into my wallet and putting a scar on my body. Why should I have an operation when your pills relieve the pain?"

I did the best I could. I talked with his wife, his children, his friends. I talked again and again with Doug. Doug would not talk—or listen.

Then came the evening when I got the call I knew was coming. It was Doug. This time the pill under his tongue wasn't working.

"Doug, I know where you live. I'll be by with an ambulance in twelve minutes. You stay out of your car!"

"Nothing doing, Doc, I'm not riding an ambulance for a little pain in my chest. We're coming right in. My wife will drive."

It's best that she was driving. Doug was dead when they arrived at the medical center.

Chapter 8

Loggers

MY FIRST SERIOUS JOB IN PITTSBURGH was in the steel mills. I had almost completed a degree in chemical engineering and found that my skills were needed by the Jones & Laughlin Steel Company.

When I came to the West, I found no open hearths, no blast furnaces, no rolling mills. I was equipped with a lot of useless skills. As I mentioned earlier, many of the people in Twisp were loggers. I had to learn a new vocabulary, a new way of life, a new attitude toward professional people.

I learned that a logger cut a *face* in the tree he was about to fall. This was an open cut made in the direction in which he hoped the tree would fall. He would then get down on his hands and knees and peer into the face to see if the tree was hollow. It frequently was. This gave him some idea about which direction he could expect the tree to fall. His next task was to make a *back cut* with his chain saw on the opposite side of the tree. This was usually shored up with the wedges he carried just for that purpose.

Eventually the tree would start to lean, usually in the direction he had originally intended. When it fell—it fell. No one shouted "Timber-r-r-r!" as I had been taught to expect in Saturday afternoon movies. The logger identified the stump as his, sawed the limbs off the tree and proceeded to cut the remaining tree (now called a log) into forty-foot lengths.

A skidder would then come by to pull the log out to the log deck where it would be stacked to await transportation to the mill. Two kinds of skidders were used: the tracked skidder on bulldozer-like tracks and the rubber-tired skidder mounted on four enormous rubber tires. The operators of these machines could work on the side of a hill either horizontally or vertically.

Recently a new device had been introduced. It was a machine with a long boom which attached itself to the tree about forty or fifty feet above the ground. An enormous circular saw then appeared from the machine's base and proceeded to cut through the trunk a few inches above the ground. Since the operator had control of the tree with his attached boom, he could lay it down anywhere it was safe and convenient to do so. The ground crew then removed the branches and cut the newly-made log into standard lengths so that they could be transported to the mill.

* * *

That's the way it was supposed to be. True to somebody's law, it didn't always work out that way and that's why they needed me. I couldn't operate any of these machines, but I knew what to do when things went wrong.

I learned early in my stay in the Methow Valley that when the woods boss called for an ambulance and suggested that "the doctor come along" he probably had a fatality. Fatal it is when a Douglas fir, thirty or more inches on the stump, falls on a logger. Our big job then is to get him out from under the tree. His fellow loggers have little stomach for the process, but it has to be done.

My first woods fatality occurred when a very experienced faller dropped a tree across one of the skid cats on which two of his friends were riding. We lost both of them. It was an honest error. The faller felt awful for the rest of his life. Remember it is noisy in the woods during logging operations. There is the sound of chain saws, of the skid cats, loading rigs, trucks taking logs to the mill and bulldozers making new roads for the next phase of the operation. All of this takes its toll on hearing acuity. If you talk to a logger in a normal conversational voice, he's likely to keep asking you to repeat what you said.

* * *

One day you will get a call to a woods injury in a falling zone. As you arrive, you notice everyone just standing around, doing nothing. That in itself tells you a lot. The woods boss approaches the ambulance and tells you that he has lost one of his men. You know most of these men. You have cared for their families and delivered their babies. Your next question is, "Who?"

On this day the reply was "Jack Prime." I knew Jack and liked him. I felt like someone had struck me in the chest with a board. I couldn't go on. I sent my ambulance crew with a few of the loggers to dig him out from under the tree. Immediately the entire crew began making excuses for Jack explaining that it wasn't his fault, that each of them had done the same thing many times, that he was just unlucky that day. There is nothing so final as the day of a death. But I had his wife and his father yet to talk with. I dreaded that. I knew them all. My crew brought him back to the ambulance discreetly zipped into a body bag. There he stayed until we delivered him to the funeral director. I didn't even make an attempt to formally identify the body. Jack had gone to work that day. He did not come home.

Talking with his wife was easier than I had expected. But his father was an engineer at Boeing in Seattle, about 250 miles away. His father knew that Jack lived a dangerous life and may have expected such a call. Nevertheless it is hard to call a father you have never met and tell him that you have just taken his son's body out from under a fallen tree.

The father said something like, "Are you trying to tell me that my son is dead?"

I answered with tears in my eyes, "Yes, sir. Jack did not survive the accident."

There are few things that I have done that were more difficult than what I did that afternoon. There are some things you should not have to do over the telephone. When you hang up you know that it is not all over. It is just beginning.

One afternoon I responded with the woods boss to an accident on Lamb Butte. Because I was with the woods boss, I assumed that I would find a recently deceased friend. This time in thirty inches of snow I found Andy Winchester. (Andy was the one who had dropped the tree across the skid cat carrying two of his friends several years earlier.) Andy had been caught by a "barber chair." This is a defect that a falling tree can develop for a host of reasons. The net result is that you don't know where the tree is going to land, and when it does the stump has a long vertical axis that makes it look like an old-fashioned barber chair.

The tree, as it fell against Andy, broke both of his legs between the ankle and the knee. All four bones (two in each leg) were protruding through the skin. I had no warning what I was going after and therefore had no equipment or supplies. The other loggers had quite adequately splinted the legs with branches they found lying around the tree.

Andy was in pain. I apologized that I had no pain medicine. He did not complain and probably he was helped by the beta endorphins which our brain supplies us in situations such as this. He did tell me that he could take it because his two friends—on that skid cat several years before—didn't get any pain medicine either. He had never forgotten that day. Andy never worked again. It took more than eight months for his legs to heal.

I have taken care of too many woods fatalities. The hardest part is realizing who the victim is. The next hardest is the visit that you, and only you, must make to the family.

Chapter 9

The Packers

THERE IS A DISTINCT GROUP OF MOUNTAIN MEN who at one time were very important to the opening of the West. These men called themselves *packers*. This meant that they talked mule talk, could handle their horses, and could move a lot a freight over trails to the logging camps and to the gold mines. These men could pack up a load of freight, wrap it in a piece of canvas, called a manty, and then position the packs on the back of a horse or a mule in a balanced fashion that would not shift on the trail. They knew every stream, every lake and every trail in the back country. They called the mountains "the hills." They ate little, drank a lot, and were indestructible. Weather might set them back a few days, but only if the snow was over four feet deep. Their great contribution to wilderness living was trail whiskey. This was usually a moonshine product from one of their stills or commercial whiskey cut half and half with water. They were a wild bunch who loved to play jokes on each other.

These men knew horses and could converse with mules. The animals were obedient to them. The animals knew if they did something wrong the packer would speak to them in mule language. The packers would be gone from their homes from the date the snow melted in the passes until the end of deer-hunting season in the fall. Most of them were married and had children.

A conspicuous characteristic of these men was their use of alcoholic beverages. They were usually drinking but could do their job in spite of the alcohol. Sometimes they had to be helped out of the saddle at the end of the day. They were deeply concerned with their livestock. The horse and the mule were their way of making a living. At the end of the day the animals came first. They were un-packed, watered, and turned out into good green pastures. Then the packers would sit around the campfire telling stories. They tended to live on black coffee and simple morsels of food. The trail whiskey kept them going. They scoffed at me when I tried to explain that no matter how you cut it, whiskey was a depressant. No, sir! On a cold day it was a life saver. "Just ask Sven. He'll tell you about the time we thawed Lucky out with trail whiskey." (If you stay with me long enough, I'll tell about that night.)

Packers are still a vital part of the existence of hunt-ers and the ever-increasing number of people who look to the hills for recreation. But most of the old-timers are gone now. They were a tough and self-reliant breed, but time has taken its toll—along with the effects of their favorite beverage, the cigarettes they smoked, the snoose they chewed, the mule kicks they sustained, and the days when they rode twenty-five miles or more in the saddle with pneumonia that should have put them in the hospital.

So much for generalizations. Let me introduce you to a few of these guys.

Chapter 10

Sven and Sparky

MY FIRST ENCOUNTER WITH THIS GROUP of 20th Century mountain men came with Sven Olsen. Sven owed me money. On the other hand, that did not make me unique. He owed everybody money. When asked for it, he would smile and tell us that in the fall when he sold his steers he would pay. In the meantime, was there anything he could do for us to show his appreciation. Sven drank a lot of trail whiskey and was a darn nice drunk. He had a lovely wife and several children. I delivered some of them. I'm not sure they were ever paid for. Now, twenty-five or thirty years later, I am delivering his grandchildren. Sven's descendants are respected members of their community.

The Olsen bill in my office was getting pretty high. Sven would say, "Thanks, Doc, for reminding me; I'll get around to it this fall. In the meantime Sparky and I would like to take you and your friends into Hidden Lakes for a vacation." Hidden Lakes are deep in the wilderness area of the North Cascades. They are about twenty miles from the trailhead and required a packer who knew how to pack a string of horses and set up camp.

To understand this you also have to know Sam Sparks (Sparky). Sparky and Sven worked together. They made a living taking hunters, vacationers, fishermen and dudes back into the mountains. They moved freight for the Forest Service. Sparky was one of the happiest drunks I've ever known—but more about him in another section.

Several of my friends and I met Sparky and Sven at the Billy Goat Corral trailhead one summer morning. We got there early, but the packers were there first because they had spent the night there. Along with Sparky and Sven was Rob, one of Sven's relatives, who also had an affinity for trail whiskey. By sun-up the boys had a head start on us, alcohol-wise. A lot of fun was being had by all—the usual horsing around, lies, expletives, and unsolicited advice. The packers considered us real dudes and that we were.

As soon as I was in my saddle, my horse ran away with me. My three packers actually rolled on the ground in laughter. Somehow I survived Old Buck's challenge and trotted back to the trailhead to see how my other friends would fare. In spite of the frivolity, the packers seemed to know what they were doing. "Go on ahead. Just follow the trail and we'll meet you in camp." I thought that maybe they knew a shortcut. There is no shortcut to Hidden Lakes. They just didn't want to share their trail whiskey with a group of Back East dudes.

Eighteen miles later, sitting around camp without food, tents, or camping gear, we heard them coming down the trail. Sparky was leading his horse because he was too drunk to get into the saddle. Rob was just about asleep— or as the drinking crowd says "about passed out." Sven was leading the string of horses and singing a bawdy cowboy song, the words of which I wish I could remember. In camp, Sven was too drunk to get out of the saddle and had to be helped down by Willy (the fire guard at Hidden Lakes). This was even more awkward when you realize that Willy was also drunk. (To Willy's great credit, he later cleaned up his life and is now the only living survivor of the four.)

I had recently left an urban existence in Pittsburgh; my two friends were from Chicago. We were now learning about the *Real West*. The packers left us one horse and went back to the trailhead the next morning. We were convinced that we were facing a "walk out" when our time was up at Hidden Lakes. But, to our surprise, Sven came back for us three days later.

Over the next fifteen years, I reduced Sven's dislocated shoulder three times, delivered his children, and sewed up his injured arms and legs when chain saws kicked back on him. I made the tearful diagnosis that he had cancer of the bladder, and I stayed with him until one fall day at home he slipped into a coma and died. He had been dry for about two years before his final ordeal. He kept on smiling and never asked for a drink.

Routinely, our business office sent him bills for professional services until one day one of the aides in my front office tore up the ledger and threw it away. I didn't protest. The cowboys and packers gave him a "proper" funeral and then toasted, in their own way, the loss of a real mountain man.

* * *

Sparky lived on. He was drunk for about two weeks after the loss of Sven. Like them all, Sparky always had a wisecrack or a grin. He was more entertaining when he was drunk. One day he told me he just couldn't stand being sober because then he could remember how good he felt when he was drunk.

Sparky was also a packer. He raised and fed a few steers which helped him pay the taxes on his "place." He preferred to be in the mountains. He spoke horse talk and understood mule dialect. He handled his horses with great skill when they were on the trail. From the time he was a Marine sergeant fighting at Guadacanal, Sparky was never without his bottle of booze.

He seemed to have a poorly controlled death wish. I saved his life about four times. Several times I pulled him out from under a damaged vehicle. I was there when he tore his thumb off in a roping accident. On one occasion I opened his abdomen and stopped a dangerous hemorrhage after he had driven his car into a fir tree. I was there when a mule kicked him. I took him to the hospital where I drained the enormous blood clot from his scrotum.

I was also there when he came to me in late April and announced that he wanted to stop drinking. When we moved over to the window for better light, I could see that he really was *yellow*. My brief comment was, "Sparky, it's too late." And it was.

While he was still in the hospital, some of his Marine platoon now living in Seattle, Tacoma, and Everett heard that "the sarge" was sick. They got into a van and, equipped with some Vodka and orange juice, traveled the 200 miles to the hospital. The nurses objected to their visit and especially their refreshments. Those old Marines paid little attention to the nurses and invaded Sparky's room for one last binge. The next week, before the rest of the old platoon could come over for another party, Sparky died with a smile on his face.

Sparky had taken me and my family into the hills on several trips. I liked him. Whether he was drunk or sober (and mostly drunk), I'd ride with him any time.

Chapter 11

Mitch

MITCH WAS A NICE GUY. A pleasant man, Mitch was a cowboy, a horse-man, a logger, a packer, a woodcutter, and one of the nicest alcoholics our valley ever produced.

He could, and would, stand his ground when harassed by his peers, but occasionally his world would experience one of his outbursts of anger and violence. Usually his friends knew just how far to push him. They had a way of stopping short. Mitch took the kidding so graciously that they were reluctant ever to hurt him. He usually ended up consuming the trail whisky that his good-natured tormentors would gladly supply. Mitch smiled and laughed a lot, at times was serious, worked hard, and drank a lot.

As a packer, his mules and horses would stand still for him. His loads were always balanced and never came loose on the trail. His animals knew him as well as he knew them. He was seldom violent toward them in any way, other than in speech. In colorful and metaphoric language, Mitch would talk to a mule and tell him he was dissatisfied with his performance. The mule, of course, would strive to do better. His horses, on the other hand, felt a superiority over Mitch. They felt that anyone who would converse with mules must be an inferior being. Yet they were loyal to him. He fed them well, watered them generously, loaded them lightly, and kept their hooves trimmed. What more could a pack horse desire?

Mitch knew our mountains. He knew where the cabins were located, the easiest passes and trails, the best browse, and the most reliable streams for water. Mitch knew hardship as well as discomfort and disappointment. When things got downright impossible, he would retreat into the hills, and there was always the bottle of trail whiskey to warm things up and help him endure.

One evening he led a string of pack horses through freezing rain and snow. When he arrived at the cabin, he found that other packers had arrived before him and had a fire going. After unloading his pack string and settling them for the night, he went into the cabin. It was then that he found that it was difficult to walk and that he couldn't sit. His clothes had absorbed the rain, and the cold wind had frozen them into a solid sheet of ice. Mitch had to stand by the fire while his friends turned him every ten minutes to thaw him out. Inside that pillar of ice stood Mitch, shivering with such intensity that his teeth chattered. All would have been lost if it had not been for the ever-present trail whiskey, which his friends poured into his mouth following each turn. Eventually he thawed, left a puddle of water on the floor, removed his clothes, had supper, and lay down to sleep in a state of pleasant intoxication.

In the morning he was stiff and cold, but otherwise no worse for the wear. He consumed the usual pint of black coffee with bacon and eggs. Before the others had found their boots, his animals were repacked and he was back on the trail.

Mitch supported his family with a wide variety of endeavors. One day there was an accident in the woods. Mitch was hurt. The accident left him with a weakened back that wouldn't heal and couldn't be fixed. From that time on, Mitch lived with pain. Usually he smiled, but at times his face would betray the agony of distorted vertebrae and compressed nerves. His whiskey, or by now his bottle of wine, did more to give him bodily comfort than could any medication offered by his physicians. He could still cut a cord or two of wood, slowly. He would cut one for his family and maybe one to sell. His woods' injury entitled him to a life-long pension from the State Industrial Compensation System. On this he lived and raised his family. With this he bought his wine.

His friends built him a house, plowed his garden, and cut his wood for winter fuel. There was always one who would go to the liquor store for him. Everybody liked Mitch and respected him as the prototype mountain man, now fallen on bad times.

In order to understand Mitch, you would have to understand Susie. Susie belonged to Mitch. They were married and had three daughters. One of the daughters had the same infectious smile and good humor as Mitch, but she never grew up. She was born with a misbuilt heart and died before she was twenty years old.

But Susie simply bubbled with enthusiasm for life and for Mitch. She adored, even worshipped, him. She was always waiting after a hard day or week in the hills. Susie wasn't the best cook in the valley but she and Mitch were never hungry. Her house was messy and seldom picked up. But houses were for eating and for sleeping, and the rest of the time a person belonged out of doors. Susie's torso had a rounded shape which doctors call truncal obesity; she had short arms and legs and wide eyes that betrayed perpetual bewilderment and awe. She was a good woman who would believe almost everything she was told. When Mitch became chronically sick with a variety of illnesses, she was constantly at his side to be his nurse and helpmate. She knew there was a cure for Mitch and that she would find it.

On a winter afternoon Mitch drove Susie to the grocery store. (He would never allow her to learn to operate anything except a tractor or a team of horses.) He took with him the brown bag that hid the bottle of whiskey to which he owed an obligation that day. As Susie shopped, Mitch sat in the car and tested the contents of the brown bag lest they spoil. Susie emerged from the store with a large bag of groceries. Just as she stepped off the curb, she slipped on the ice; her foot was caught in the space between the front left tire of the car and the curb of the sidewalk. She fell with a howl and scattered groceries over the parking lot.

Mitch took another sip from his brown bag and expected her to get up so that they could go on home. (Mitch later confessed to me that he was too drunk to stand or walk, but driving a car he could do.) Susie did not get up. Her leg developed a grotesque appearance. She had, in fact, dislocated her knee. This is a serious injury that frequently damages blood vessels and nerves. The result, all too often, is an amputation of the leg.

Emergency care, there on the shopping center pavement, was performed properly by a young pharmacist. The ambulance arrived and Susie had a ride to the nearest orthopedic surgeon (a distance of about 100 miles). The leg was surgically stabilized but I was fearful of the final result. I have cared for this injury before. The knee healed. She kept her leg.

The healing process required that she be in a plaster cast that immobilized her entire leg, hip, and lower abdomen. When I would visit her at home, I found her in this cast that extended from her mid abdomen to the tips of the left toes. She could barely walk and couldn't sit. Yet she slept on the couch in the living room about twelve feet from the hospital bed that had been set up for Mitch. When we suggested that she would be more comfortable in her own bed, I was reminded that the bedroom had no heat and, anyway, she had to be close to Mitch in the event that he needed her during the night. She was convinced that without her constant attention Mitch would die. In spite of her cast she was true to this personal commitment and it could not be otherwise.

Mitch's health began to deteriorate. The demands upon me for house calls escalated to about four times a week. Mitch would experience "attacks." During these attacks he would choke, clutch at his chest and neck, and be convulsed with apprehension and fear. He would even turn blue. Susie was terrified. Each time he had an attack, she was convinced she was witnessing his last breath. If you had ever seen these attacks, you would join her in this thought. For several years she would have a friend drive Mitch to the nearest hospital, which was forty miles away. There a doctor would see him. His treatment was always effective.

Now, these attacks made no sense medically, but they

were always controlled with an injection of Demerol. The doctor would keep Mitch overnight in the hospital because he really didn't know what was going on. The next morning, covered with clean white sheets, a freshly laundered blanket and enjoying a breakfast in bed, Mitch would be all smiles. Finally the doctor told Susie that these attacks were "heart attacks." What a relief! She finally had a diagnosis, albeit a dangerous diagnosis. It was one that she could relate to. (A "non-diagnosis" she could not respond to with any emotion other than fear and anxiety.)

Susie began to keep score. I entered into Mitch's routine care at about the eighth "heart attack." I couldn't confirm that diagnosis, but the family was content with that one, so I didn't change it. Mitch's electrocardiograms were always normal. The attacks continued to occur at six-to-eight week intervals. I still had no good working diagnosis, but the pattern was set. Susie knew that I knew the way to their home. She knew that I carried the wonder drug that would cure Mitch, and I always played my part according to the script.

Susie would call me usually in a state of panic about the time I would be going to bed or shortly thereafter. I always responded. I remember cold nights, wet nights, nights full of snow. I remember putting chains on my car so that I could get home after a house call to Mitch's. And always, one small shot of Demerol restored Mitch to peace and comfort. I questioned myself about the use of this narcotic, but the intervals between Mitch's attacks were so long that I discounted the possibility of drug dependency.

One night, after a particularly successful "save," Susie was fluttering about in absolute joy over my success. She approached me in sincere appreciation. A voice inside me said, "Be careful, she is going to kiss you." She did. I smiled, did not return the honor, and made a gentlemanly attempt to escape from the house. But I was foiled again. The door knob was covered with Bag Balm; it slipped in my hand rather than turning to unlatch the door. This pause gained me another kiss and a hug. The hug from Susie, whose hands were also covered with Bag Balm, deposited a large residue on the back of my shirt. (Bag Balm is a proprietary combination of mineral salve and carbolic acid originally compounded to treat the infected udder of a milk cow. It is now used throughout rural America for everything from skin ulcers to lubrication on tractors and faucets. Mitch felt that it helped him breathe a bit easier when Susie rubbed it on his chest.)

After I succeeded in opening the door and going forth into the night, I reflected that few big-city doctors ever experience appreciation delivered so spontaneously and with such fervor.

In addition to his attacks, Mitch was now developing chronic bronchitis with a profuse discharge of sputum from the lungs. Doctors call this bronchorrhea. Mitch called it spit. It must be coughed up or its formation must be suppressed. The first Mitch was good at; the latter I was a failure at. Mitch carried his spit can with him everywhere he went. In the waiting room of my office he would wheeze, cough, and spit in a somewhat disgusting manner. Seldom did my office staff permit Mitch to spend much time in our waiting room. He was always moved rapidly to an exam room where he could handle his secretions in some privacy.

I was now faced with a dilemma. If Mitch should have

one of his "heart attacks" while his lungs were acting up, the Demerol I gave him for the attack would decrease his cough response. This would allow secretions to build up in his lungs and possibly result in pneumonia. Mitch, however, didn't need my help. He developed pneumonia on his own at increasingly frequent intervals. These always merited a trip to the hospital. During one of these trips, I discovered that Mitch now had an insulin dependent diabetes mellitus. This required at least one and sometimes two insulin injections a day, along with some modification of the diet and alcohol intake. Mitch and Susie could manage the insulin injections, but there was no change in his intake of food or alcohol.

I would like you to picture Mitch as he was in his home. A hospital bed had been moved into the front room. A therapist had fitted the head end of the bed with a traction device that Mitch would use when his neck bothered him. At the foot end of the bed was another traction apparatus that Mitch would use when his low back bothered him. Overhead was a stationary bar and a trapeze that enabled him to move about in bed. Next to the bed was the tank of oxygen and the vaporizer apparatus from which Mitch took his respiratory therapy treatments. To the left of the bed was a table that supported, in addition to the current spit can, a host of pill bottles. Mitch never threw out a single prescription bottle. I found him to be taking about ten prescription preparations. He knew the name of each preparation, its purpose, and its frequency. Some of the medicines were not in my records but were holdovers from his doctor's care five years previously. Among this mess was an insulin syringe designed for single use. But Susie, in an attempt to save money, and knowing nothing of the germ theory, used it twice a day for at least a week before changing to a new syringe.

Here Mitch would lie for hours, breathing steam, traction applied to his neck and low back, reading Zane Grey novels about the Old West. Susie would sit nearby, always ready to jump to his most trivial demand or request. Through it all Mitch kept his grip on the wine bottle, which his well-meaning friends always brought with them when they came to visit. Susie didn't like that but was powerless to prevent it.

Mitch had many doctors. We were all bewildered by his failing health and our futile attempts to control his decline. One day an ambulance took him to a large hospital in a distant city. There he died and we know not why.

This man simply burned out. Disease, poor nutrition, diabetes, and alcohol have their price. For Mitch the misery of living exceeded the peace of dying. So, he died.

Chapter 12

Smoke Jumpers

IN MY NAVY DAYS I worked closely with the pilots and enlisted men who made our squadron operational. When I arrived in the Methow Valley, I found the civilian equivalent of the military squadron I had just left. These were the North Cascade Smoke Jumpers.

They are a group of young men who are trained and equipped to approach a forest fire from the sky. If they jumped a fire soon enough, a few of these young experts can control or even put out a fire that threatens an entire forest. This is dangerous work. It requires a very high level of training and physical fitness, which is based upon historical incidents in which things went right—and wrong.

These men would approach a fire from an aircraft at about 1,500 feet above the tops of the trees. They jumped, carrying working gear and survival gear. Their parachutes were steerable, but because of the low jump they had little time to adjust their rate of descent to comply with prevailing winds and up drafts from the fire. Once on the ground, they went to work assembling their gear and then attacking the fire. Often a ground crew was sent to the fire zone to help them and perhaps relieve them of the primary control of the fire. In this way, several of the jumpers could be sent out to two or three fires a day. Unless they were brought out by helicopter, they had to pack all of their gear out on their own backs. This would consist of their primary chute, the reserve chute, the hard hat, the jump suit, and whatever equipment was dropped for them to use in attacking the fire. Such a load could weigh more than one hundred pounds.

The smoke jumpers have an enviable record. There have been no fatalities in this area. There have been some serious injuries but no legs or arms are missing.

In my time supporting these activities, we had some scares and some serious injuries. There was a time in 1970 that a Forest Service helicopter took me in to the fire line at Peeve Creek. The previous night a burning snag (a dead tree set ablaze by the forest fire) had fallen across a jumper's chest and shoulder. His friends managed to release him. They thought he had a fracture of the clavicle, fractures of several ribs, possibly a collapsed lung, and probably a dislocated shoulder. He was covered with blankets to keep the burning debris from falling on him and treated at the scene with generous amounts of Demerol, a narcotic from the boss smoke jumper's first aid kit.

When I arrived the next morning at about 0700, the forest was still on fire. Burning trees were falling without warning all around me. I became a bit apprehensive, not only for the injured smoke jumper but also for myself. On the fire line there is a strange odor that only those who have been there can understand. It is indescribable—this combined with the realization that a tree burning only twenty feet away from me had fallen without warning.

I did a cursory examination of the injured firefighter and became apprehensive over his continued stay in what I was quickly learning was a dangerous place.

A small Hughes helicopter was in a clearing about fifty yards away. A stretcher was rigged on the right set of skids in what I learned to call M*A*S*H style. We put the injured man in this stretcher. I got into the right seat of the helicopter. You will appreciate my anxiety when I realized that in this position I could not monitor the patient's vital signs, especially his level of consciousness. In addition, I didn't have much confidence that my pilot knew his way to the fire camp.

Nevertheless, amidst the smoke and stench of the fire, amidst my anxiety over the welfare of the injured smoke jumper out there on the skids, and amidst a lot of highly effective prayer, we became airborne. The pilot, with a chart of the area on his knees, rapidly found the fire camp, and we transferred the injured jumper to a bigger helicopter.

There was one more thing that I failed to share with anyone else. It was my opinion that this man had a pneumothorax. A pneumothorax places a bolus of air between the lung, where it should be, and the chest wall, where it shouldn't be. As you ascend in altitude, the volume of air increases, and in so doing interferes with the return of blood to the chest and the delivery of air to the other lung. It was necessary that my pilot keep as low as possible and stay in the valleys rather than going up over the mountain ridges. We flew straight to the hospital in Wenatchee, about 140 miles to the south. This new pilot made a marvelous landing in the parking lot of the hospital, and the patient was rushed to the emergency room. After very competent evaluation, we all agreed that this jumper would soon jump again. His injuries were not as serious as we all had thought.

* * *

Another smoke jumper story happened the next day on the same fire. It illustrates the amazing resilience of the American male—especially the young American male.

I received a call from the same duty officer who had called me out the previous morning.

"Can you be ready to go back to Peeve Creek again?"

"Yes. When do we leave and what am I going for?"

"First light." (It was now 4 a.m.) "It's another bad injury. Can you be ready at the airport in fifteen minutes?"

I was there. We flew in to the same fire camp. This time a small Bell helicopter brought my patient out to me. He had jumped onto a grove of trees the previous night. His chute had hung up on a dead tree and the tree broke under his weight. He had fallen about sixty feet, feet first, to the ground. His right leg was now three inches shorter than his left leg. He could not move it.

"Hello. I'm Dr. Henry. I hear that you have had a bad night."

"Hi. I'm John Nieman." Then, with a genuine smile, he added, "What's for breakfast?"

"John, that will have to wait for a while. Let's run down to the hospital and take a few pictures first."

"Okay. How far is the hospital? I'm starved."

"About sixty miles, but with a bird like this we can make it in an hour."

John had a hip fracture. The main shaft of the femur, the straight portion of the hip bone, was broken where it angles into the hip joint and was driven up into the soft tissue of the side of his pelvic musculature. A more forceful fall might have driven it up into his armpit. This type of fracture is notorious for its internal bleeding. John's was no exception. We had to replace three pints of blood before we could begin the orthopedic surgery necessary to achieve a proper reduction of the fracture. During the procedure he received another pint of blood. Clinically, Joe showed NO SHOCK.

The next morning we gave him his breakfast.

John came back the next year with the hardware out of his hip. He re-qualified as a smoke jumper and spent a good summer jumping on fires.

The first man was unnecessarily narcotized. Demerol is a powerful narcotic that can do more harm than good if it's administered too generously. Because today's smoke jumpers receive much more training in emergency medicine than they received in 1970, this would not happen now.

Chapter 13

Hunting Accidents

PEOPLE WANT TO HELP. People want to be useful to others. This is called caring, and it doesn't carry a price tag. People want to help other people—even strangers—because they like to do it.

The weather was clear and cold. The fall hunting season was in progress. Our trails and valleys were crowded with hunters and adventurers seeking an out-of-doors experience before the winter snows fell. Our valley's large deer population brought a herd of hunters and visitors from the cities of Washington.

The modern hunter takes his hobby seriously. He arms himself with expensive weaponry. There always seems to be a four-by-four vehicle with roll bar and CB antennas. There is the inevitable gun rack over the rear window of the cab. Many are wearing camouflage clothing. A few still bring their whiskey, playing cards, poker chips, and girl friends. Most come to hunt and are serious outdoors men.

The hunter prepares for the hunt. We prepare for the hunter.

Those of us who have been involved in emergency services know that a significant number of these hunters will not be prepared for their wilderness challenge. They get lost. They forget about the severity of our weather or the distortions of landmarks brought on by wind, rain and snow.

Those who are lost usually walk out somewhere and create their own self-rescue. Those who are hurt need help. You would have to experience the distress of a sprained ankle, alone, at night, on or off the trail in wooded terrain to appreciate the helpless feeling a stranger to the woods will experience. The forest will suddenly become hostile. Your imagination will remind you of all of the media stories about attacks by bears and cougars. Survival becomes your major preoccupation, and fear will reign.

We all live with the fantasy of personal indestructibility and self-sufficiency. Yet these qualities, of which we are so proud, are seldom tested. When they are tested, we are terrified by the reality of our own limitations and weaknesses.

Wilderness expeditions are not for weekend athletes. Usually we are rescuing competent hunters, qualified rock climbers, experienced skiers. They are good at what they do. But they are seldom ready when the wilderness furnishes a test of their capabilities. Some fight, some cope, some think. Many become passive and just sit down to wait it out. Few there are who ever find that the good Lord has blessed us with a second wind, and a third, and a fourth.

After many years of working on wilderness rescues, we have developed a few rules of thumb that assist us in planning and carrying out our missions:

1. The request for a rescue will come at night.
2. It will be raining or snowing.
3. Everyone wants to help.
4. Everyone who wants to help will graciously yield to competent leadership.

Such was a night in October. All that was lacking was the rain, but I guess there are always exceptions. At about 11 p.m., I was informed that Paul Bryant had been shot in the leg and was lying in a tent awaiting our care. The tent was eight miles from the Rattlesnake Camp trailhead in the vicinity of Hart's Pass. Our rescue wheels moved quickly. Within fifteen minutes I had collected about twelve rescuers at our rescue base in Twisp. Some woman, on her own initiative, had packed some sandwiches and cookies for us. From the Forest Service there appeared powerful portable radios. Billy Flagg appeared with a horse, and Claude Miller met us at the trailhead with several more horses and saddles.

Bob Ulrich and I were the rescue leaders, so we got the horses. Billy Flagg took the lead with our portable, collapsible stretcher across his lap in the saddle. The stretcher was in two half-shell parts with four detachable handles. Somehow Billy managed these pieces and his horse. Another rescuer followed on foot carrying the wheel that made the stretcher into an alpine wheelbarrow. If there was a moon, it never penetrated into our dark valley. The trail followed along a headwater of the Methow River which is called Rattlesnake Creek. We used no lights. Our wrangler led us, trusting to the innate thing called horse sense. He trusted that the lead horse would find the way by feel and wilderness intuition. Bob and I were uncomfortable with this blind dependence on a mere horse. Yet Billy, as the boss wrangler, insisted that we keep our lights darkened.

We moved as rapidly as we could. We did not talk. The noise of the river on our left made conversation difficult. It was a pleasant night, a bit cold. It was a night canopied by a magnificent display of stars. In the forested parts of the trail, it was very dark. The horses led us on and seemed to know what they were doing.

After about six miles, the conditions did not improve. We were on a narrow part of the trail with a steep bank on our right and the river on our left. We heard noise and confusion ahead. The lead horse had fallen into the river. First there was a loud equine protest from a surprised horse. Then our wrangler made a loud, eloquent protest from the middle of the stream. His comments regarding the horse's genealogy were classic and impressive. Amidst all of this splashing and chaos was the sound of our aluminum stretcher and poles colliding with rocks and tree trunks as they washed on downstream in the dark. Bob and I managed to retrieve all the parts with the help of our flashlights and our willingness to wade in and get wet. In a remarkably short time we were back in the saddle and on the trail again.

The remainder of the rescue team were on the trail behind us hiking in with the food and supplies for a major rescue. They never knew about the water incident. We never told.

At a wide spot in the trail, eight miles and two hours after we started, we found a tent, the injured man, and a companion. Paul was wrapped in sleeping bags in the tent. A gentle fire kept the entry to the tent reasonably warm.

Paul was conscious, very pale, and somewhat apprehensive. There was little pain. He complained of a cold leg.

It was important to me to reconstruct the accident so that I could understand the extent of the injury. The previous evening Paul had been returning from a day of hunting. He had not been successful. In addition to his hunting rifle, he carried a .357 magnum revolver attached to a holster on his right hip. In that weapon were live rounds of ammunition, one of which was in the barrel under the hammer. As he had worked his way through a stand of dense underbrush, a branch caught the trigger and fired the gun. The resulting discharge drove a bullet through Paul's leg just above the knee. There was intense pain for an instant as he fell forward. He was not able to get up. The pain was immediately replaced with a feeling of cold. The surrounding ground and his clothes were covered with blood. He could not move. His friends had heard the shot, searched for him, and eventually found him. They carried him to the tent and one of them went for help.

Bob and I were the first rescuers at the camp. While Billy Flagg attended to his horses, we examined Paul. Our first impression was that he had suffered a significant blood loss. We removed his clothes and looked at the leg. It was still *there!* The leg was cold and I could find no pulse at the ankle. At the level of the knee the leg was still attached with strands of skin, tendon, and ligament. The nerve was severed and the bleeding had stopped due to the shock. The leg had functionally been blown off the body. Structurally it was still attached, but only by strands of tissue.

Paul's shock did not permit him to assist in his own

rescue. Bob and I realized the seriousness of the situation. We were eight miles from the trailhead, on a cold night, with a patient in deep shock from an almost-amputated leg.

"The leg is gone," Bob whispered.

"Let's take care of him and worry about the leg later," was my whispered reply.

Someone built another fire. The existing one was stoked to burn more brightly to give us more heat and some light. We pulled Paul partially out of the tent to get at his arms. His blood pressure was barely detectable. Bob got a needle into a vein for an intravenous infusion. I got a needle into another vein and started an infusion of dextran. (This is a solution which at that time was considered to be an effective blood/plasma substitute.) We allowed both of these lines to run wide open in hopes of expanding the blood volume and to replace, for a while, that which was on the ground.

The leg had stopped bleeding. The protective clots were secure. As Paul's blood pressure began to recover, the leg did not begin to bleed. I packed hot stones from one of the fireplaces around Paul to add some heat to his hypothermic body. I insulated the stones with one of the sleeping bags in which he was wrapped.

Gradually, Paul's color improved and his blood pressure approached normal. His first words to us were to complain of pain in his back. His back? We found that one of our hot stones had burned through the sleeping bag and was now working on his almost-bare back. We prevented a skin burn, but the sleeping bag, alas, would no longer keep any hunter warm on a cold night.

Our next discussion revolved about what we should

do about the leg. We could, with a pair of scissors and a bit of local anesthesia, remove it. Paul was in no mood to discuss this option at this time in this place. There is something too final about giving a stranger permission to remove your leg out on the trail.

So—we casted the leg in place. To move Paul with a partially detached leg would have been difficult, painful, and a bit macabre. We had plaster of Paris casting tapes, so we made a long leg cast that held the leg in place in its anatomic position. There was no pain, because there was no nerve.

We gave Paul some morphine and placed him on the stretcher. For the next five hours we walked, carried, and rolled the stretcher while Paul slept.

Paul's carry-out was harder on the crew than it was on him. Once at the trailhead an ambulance took him to Twisp, and there we met a helicopter that took him on to definitive treatment at a hospital. Here the harsh reality of the injury could be more quietly and professionally evaluated and treated.

Paul Bryant now has a new leg. He can't run. It doesn't hurt. When it wears out, he can get a new one. He has not resumed his hunting hobby.

Many people had a hand in this rescue. None of us had ever heard of Paul Byrant before. No one knew him. Few ever saw him again. He said thanks in a quiet and sincere way. He never did know how many people responded to help him. We didn't keep score. My best guess is that more than thirty people (and three horses) turned out to help a stranger who was hurt.

Chapter 14

Rescue on Liberty Bell

HIGH IN THE NORTH CASCADE MOUNTAIN RANGE there is a massif called Liberty Bell. It is a cluster of rock pinnacles that includes Lexington, Concord, and the Early Winter Spires as well as the distinctly shaped Liberty Bell. Mountain climbers come to our valley from all over the West to climb Liberty Bell. Often there are several parties at some stage of climb or descent on this peak.

In mid-afternoon I received a call that there was an injured climber on the summit of Liberty Bell.

The medical and humanitarian aspects of mountain rescue yield to the fact that each county sheriff has jurisdiction of all search and rescue activities in his county. This rescue presented us with a political challenge. The boundary between Okanogan County (our county) and Chelan County passes over Liberty Bell's highest point. The local sheriff's dispatcher was hesitant to order us to the rescue. The site was about 150 miles from the office and resources of the Chelan County sheriff, while we were about twenty-eight miles away, equipped with supplies, ropes, and know-how. All afternoon we argued with two sheriffs' dispatchers citing the rapid approach of night and the reported severity of the injury (open fractures of the tibia and fibula) as well as the obvious difficulty of the rescue. We and the injured climber were in the middle of a political jurisdictional dispute.

How we solved the jurisdictional issue is not part of this story. The climber, with potentially fatal shock, had to spend the night at 7,500 feet on a bare mountain top with no water and minimal protection from the weather. The next morning our climbers joined with a rescue unit from Chelan County. We put five climbers on top of that mountain by 9 a.m. Included in that team was an emergency department physician from a hospital in Wenatchee. It was a competent, well-led, and highly-trained crew. Their rescue boss was a sergeant from the sheriff's office who had had experience managing such rescues in Vietnam. Our crew became the logistics support team.

As we waited at the base of Liberty Bell, my daughter Cindy (our lead rescue paramedic) and I noticed a dark cloud to the west over Mt. Baker. It spelled trouble. We got off the mountain with the excuse that if the injured person was to be airlifted, someone had to be at the medical center to receive him. We ran down the trail. It was going to rain, and it did.

Meanwhile, on the mountain, the rescue crew made the patient comfortable, started an intravenous drip to combat shock, and administered an antibiotic to the injured climber. Then, on the mountain top, they put a cast on the broken leg from his toes to his groin. This is a superb method of stabilizing a fracture when you anticipate a difficult evacuation.

The helicopter, which came from Seattle (about 250

miles), put down in a nearby pass to wait out the approaching storm. With that storm came thunder, and before each crash of thunder, there was lightning. There are no words to describe that storm. When Cindy and I reached the parking lot at the trailhead, we looked back up at the summit. It was glowing with blue static. With lights flashing and sirens blowing, we left the scene to take up station at the medical center in Twisp, twenty-eight miles to the south.

The climbers on the mountain top were exposed to it all. Every one of the climbers, including the injured person, received at least two hits of lightning. No one died. All had some lasting effect to remind them to stay out of a thunder storm. Some had femoral nerve neuritis. One experienced a fibrillation of his respiratory muscles. He couldn't breathe. He survived. Some felt as if the shock traveled up from the peak to the clouds above, using their wet clothes as a lightning rod.

The rescue crew removed the victim from the aluminum stretcher and found a tiny foxhole for him to hide in on the edge of the peak. The leader of the crew took a hit that caused all of his trunk muscles to violently contract. This caused him to make a huge, involuntary jump. He lay down. The summit of the mountain is so small that another jump might have sent him off the top of the peak.

Eventually it all calmed down. The bushes gave off a glow of static electricity that reminded one of the members of the crew of a passage in the Bible. Moses stood on a mountain top and observed a bush that was burning but was not being consumed. God spoke to Moses through that bush. The crew now believe they have seen the bush. They also noticed the static electricity climbing their descent ropes.

It was with a great deal of apprehension that they rappelled down that rope, using no metallic let-down devices.

The helicopter came. It was windy. The down draft from the rotors made things worse. The crew was able to shove the patient and stretcher into the back compartment of the helicopter while it hovered with only one skid on the summit. The pilot did not wait around to supply taxi service to the rest of the crew. He arrived at the medical center in Twisp at about the same time that Cindy and I drove in with our ambulance.

We were able to get an x-ray through the cast of the injured leg. The bones were fractured but were in good position. It was a dangerous injury that demanded operative intervention by orthopedic surgeons. We administered a tetanus shot and loaded the patient back into the helicopter with dry clothes and blankets. Since the helicopter was going back to Seattle, there was no reason to make a land ambulance trip.

The victim survived. He has a good leg. I don't know whether he has resumed his climbing career. The crew from Wenatchee survived with a host of stories to tell about the rescue. They made one thing clear to me: "The next time you have a complex rescue on a mountain top, please do it yourself, Doctor."

Chapter 15

Animals *and* Their Owners

THE PRINCIPLES OF VETERINARY MEDICINE were never presented to us in medical school. But certain principles apply to all mammals whether they walk on two legs or four. I was often asked to minister to a hurt animal, because the Methow Valley at that time had no resident veterinarian.

One night a Pekinese dog was brought in that had had a sad encounter with a cat. The cat had taken a swipe at the curious dog with one of its claws. The assault resulted in a rupture of the dog's right eye. This is a dangerous injury. When I found that the globe and the cornea had been penetrated and that the thick gelatinous fluid within the eye was escaping, I realized there was but one treatment. The eye had to be removed.

Such an operation brings the danger of infection, tetanus being the major risk. There is also the risk of sympathetic ophthalmia. This is a poorly understood phenomenon, wherein the good eye will sympathetically lose sight in a matter of days. I had been present at the surgical enucleation of an eye in my training, and I had reviewed the training films describing how to do the procedure. Anesthesia was the first concern, and I accomplished that with an injection behind the eye. The removal is not easy if you want to do it right and remain friends with the family and the dog. The nearest ophthalmologist was 100 miles away. I removed the eye. It bled a bit; then all was dry and quiet. Putting any semblance of a bandage on the face of a Pekinese is impossible.

Since the family was from Seattle, about 250 miles away, I suggested that in the very near future they find someone who really knew what was to be expected. Through it all, the little dog sat with his front legs crossed and expressed disdain that the procedure took so long. He never protested.

* * *

Dogs with porcupine quills in their muzzles are an ever-present problem. It is usually a big dog, not at all willing to lie still. The dog is constantly scratching at his face. Many times the dog cannot close his mouth because of quills in the tongue and throat. (Dogs never attack another animal with their mouths closed.)

My first quill patient was a German shepherd. He was convinced that I was his assailant. This calls for general anesthesia. There was no operating room. I refused to take the dog into my emergency room. I used a drug called Ketamine, which I had never used on a dog. I took a guess at the German shepherd's weight, and then, with some help from the owner, injected the drug.

We let the dog run while the drug took effect. This it did, starting with the back legs. The dog continued to run, but the back legs just dragged along, giving no help. Eventually the animal went down, but he never closed his eyes.

We had about two minutes to remove the quills. With three of us working, the task was accomplished. Throughout the surgery, the dog howled but did not fight.

From what I know about that drug, the dog was on a psychedelic trip. The dog's eyes watched every move. Quickly he regained control of the front legs and then the back legs. Then he started exploring the fence line while his brain regained competency.

They say that once a dog tangles with a porcupine he will avoid the animal forever. Don't believe it. In a month the German shepherd was back with more porcupine quills. (I think he liked the anesthesia and wanted another trip.)

* * *

Every town has a Cat Lady. Ours was Agnes. These are ladies who like cats and raise them in great quantity. In the winter the cats have the run of the house. I have known at least two women who kept no fewer than twenty-five cats in their homes. Agnes was under my care for non-Hodgkin's lymphoma. This is a quietly malignant disease. We can supervise some of the treatment at home. Agnes insisted on it because she had to feed her cats.

When she broke her hip, I made a house call. She lived in a trailer at the edge of town. When I entered the house, I was overcome by a powerful odor. Since she did not let the cats go outside, they urinated on the carpet. Agnes was in bed. In bed with her was a dying cat. She felt that it was beneficial to the cat if it was close to her. It was not. Another cat was in the bathtub, dead. It had been sick, so she placed it in the tub as a sort of solitary confinement to keep it away from the other cats. One had died several days earlier. Since the ground was frozen, she couldn't take it outside for a cat burial, so she put it in the deep freeze. I wouldn't sit in any of her chairs. There were still about twenty other cats occupying the furniture.

It was apparent that she would have to have an ambulance ride to the hospital for care of her hip. The ambulance crew entered the house and immediately turned away and went back out onto the porch. I had to explain to the crew that they were in no danger. Later that day I called the police, and they called the Humane Society to come and retrieve as many cats as they could find. What they did with them I have no idea. The house was cleaned up when Agnes got home. She soon had to go to a nursing home because she could no longer take care of herself.

Two weeks later, when I last was involved, I overheard the law enforcement people talking about the propriety and legality of towing the trailer out of town and setting fire to it. No one could live in that trailer.

* * *

Another animal concern was the treatment of my own dog, Loki. Loki was a prime alpha in our town. He was a Norwegian elkhound. One day when the meat packing plant was disposing of scraps to the town dogs, Loki got into a jurisdictional dispute with a newcomer who also thought he was prime alpha. In the ensuing dogfight, Loki suffered a significant partial circumcision. The neighbors called the ambulance.

Loki would not allow us to carry him, so he walked over and jumped, quite painfully, into the patient compartment. I gave the poor dog a significant dose of morphine. I didn't know how to calculate dosage for a Norwegian elkhound, but it worked. Loki became almost comatose. We strapped him to a backboard and carried him into my emergency room. Injecting the local anesthesia was easy.

My assistant expressed a bit of anxiety about how we would remove the sutures. We solved that problem by using absorbable sutures, which the poor dog removed himself. It was a good repair and cosmetically acceptable. It didn't interfere with his future use of the appended organ.

* * *

Everybody knew Joe Steele, a neighbor to the medical center. He was an old cowboy who had made a barely adequate living working steers. Joe was a dirty old man. I speak not of his moral standards but of his hygienic appearance. He lived in a one-room cabin without an indoor toilet or running water. Each day he made several trips to town for his meals and to use the bathroom at the local cafe.

When Joe would drop into my office, he didn't spend much time in the waiting room. The receptionists saw to it that he quickly had an examination room all to himself. The aroma tended to make my other patients congregate on the opposite side of the room.

Joe thought that since he could talk cow talk he was superior to me. He was. He would approach me with the authority of a wise old man. He would tell me to sit down and listen to him. (I guess that's a lesson all doctors should pay attention to.) An accident I had suffered in 1975 deprived me of my olfactory nerve, my sense of smell. My staff wondered how I could spend so much time with Joe. I couldn't smell, but my eyes did water a bit while he talked. I thought he was a fascinating piece of the Old West who never accepted the 20th Century.

I am placing Joe's small vignette in the animal section

because he sat at the interface between man and steer. He had a unique way of talking to his animals. It was loud and it was profane. Furthermore, it was creative. I was called to his barnyard one Sunday morning because he was down and couldn't get up. He had been kicked by one of his horses. When I arrived, that horse was still attached by a lead rope to the upper bar of the fence. However, that upper bar of the fence was no longer attached to the fence—a somewhat bizarre problem that the horse didn't understand. So, the horse was dancing around in the corral trying to escape from the bar.

Fortunately, a neighbor who was animal-wise managed to control this part of the situation. As I approached Joe, sitting in the snow, propped up against his tack shop, I noticed that a bull was also in the cast of players. The bull, who was about twenty feet away, was looking at us with his head down, moving it back and forth. Now, Joe had a reputation for not keeping the kindest bulls in the valley, and here was one of them. Joe was talking to the bull and throwing snowballs at him. The bull seemed to understand Joe but didn't understand my intrusion.

The bull made a slight move in our direction. Joe (with his hip broken) took his left arm and struck the side of building with great force to emphasize his message to the bull. This caused an avalanche. Two feet of snow had collected on the roof, and it now cascaded down to cover Joe and me. The neighbor took care of the bull. I was convulsed in laughter, as were the other members of my rescue crew. Joe was infuriated and screamed at the animal, saying bad things about the bull's parentage.

All of this must be understood in the context that Joe at that time was seventy-eight years old. When we managed to get him into the emergency room of my medical center, the well-meaning and caring family began to gather. A sister-in-law asked what I had done with Joe's coat. Without much forethought I told her that the coat was standing over there in the corner. I immediately felt that this might be interpreted as a disrespectful comment. But it was true. The coat was standing without support in the corner of the emergency room.

Joe went to the hospital and had his hip surgically stabilized. There is much more to tell about this old man. Most amazing, perhaps, is the fact he wrote up his life stories with the help of a local writer and published them. His stories were much appreciated by the locals.

Joe lived for many years after the surgical repair. He continued to walk to town every day, a round trip of about a mile. Then one morning he was found dead in his front yard. There was no dramatic terminal event. His life was over, and so he died.

Chapter 16

Babies

WHEN I RELIVE THE YEARS of my idealistic childhood and development, I remember that the primary image I had of a doctor was that he delivered babies. For some reason I felt that obstetrics and sick kids was what a doctor did for a living. I didn't know about all the hearts and stomachs and kidneys that they also must pay attention to.

During my third year in medical school I had the opportunity to get into the delivery room and even deliver a few babies. I glowed in the realization that I was at last getting to do what doctors do. I was thrilled. I was also saddened. They didn't tell me at first about the pediatric and obstetric tragedies that can occur in the delivery room. Sometimes babies are stillborn. Some babies are malformed. Mothers experience ruptured uteri or may have severe hemorrhages right there in the delivery room. Babies are not always positioned correctly by nature for an uneventful delivery. These babies require operative intervention by the obstetrician. I learned all of these things during my third year in medical school, although most of the deliveries that I attended resulted in healthy babies and happy mothers. I thought this was stimulating and rewarding. Most important, it taught me that obstetrics demanded of me a level of skill which, at that time, I had not yet attained.

During my fourth year of medical school I continued to work for a hospital after hours and centered my interest in the department of obstetrics. This hospital had three hundred deliveries a month, which translated into ten a day for an idealistic medical student. I graduated from medical school having delivered or assisted in the delivery of 145 babies. Five years in the U.S. Navy gave me the opportunity for more experience in obstetrics. On at least one duty shift (twelve hours) I delivered five babies for Navy wives. I continued to learn from these experiences so that by the time I was ready to enter into private medical practice I possessed the confidence and skill to deliver my patients' babies.

All of this experience was in hospitals. In private rural practice in the North Cascade mountains, I did not always have the luxury of a hospital. I learned that babies come into this world when the baby has decided to come into this world. Over the next few years I found it necessary to deliver babies in ambulances, cars, dining rooms, living rooms, my office, etc. I could not ignore a call from a woman in labor.

In the 60s and 70s there developed a trend in our society to decrease the doctor's prerogatives in the delivery process. Mothers did not want birth-easing procedures such as episiotomies. (An episiotomy is an incision made between a group of muscles that enlarges the opening through which the baby's head must travel. It speeds up the delivery, decreases pain and saves the mother from development of pelvic muscle herniation of the bladder later in life.) The episiotomy is immediately repaired approximating normal tissue to normal tissue with absorbable suture. In addition to this I found a reticence on the part of some mothers to agree to accept medications or procedures designed to reduce pain of labor. I actually found some women who objected to the use of medications to control the bleeding that follows many deliveries.

* * *

Obstetrically-oriented medical personnel like it clean. We wear gowns, gloves, hats and masks. We drape the mother to keep ambient environmental germs away from our field. We not only wash our hands, we scrub them before putting on the gloves. Once the gloves are on, we touch nothing but the mother and the baby. This is how we are taught. When we work outside the hospital scene, we still take all of this with us. It is built into our behavior. It is called sterile technique and has to be learned. We are very protective of the technique.

* * *

Phyllis was a young bride. She became pregnant and glowed in her accomplishment. She would soon have her own baby.

"What is this?" she asked herself one day. "Something is happening to me. I feel a strange tension in my abdomen—it makes me want to stand still and not move. There. It's over."

But that tension comes again. It is no stronger but it lasts longer. Then it goes away. It is happening at five-minute intervals.

"I feel a strange pressure in my back. This is strange. It is almost like I am going to have my baby, but my doctor told me that that shouldn't happen for another month."

Suddenly, in the midst of one of the back pains, she feels a pop and strange gray water escapes. Now she feels less tension but the pains return. They are more severe and make her bear down.

I received a call from an anxious grandmother-to-be. It was one o'clock in the morning. An inch of new snow was on the road. Phyllis lived on the Lower Bear Creek road about six miles north of my home. It took no imagination for me to decide what was happening. On the way I picked up my nurse, Eileen, who had helped with several home deliveries (but never for a premature labor).

We arrived in time. Eileen arranged Phyllis on the bed and I opened my birthing kit. It was an easy delivery. A four-pound baby doesn't take up much room. My biggest concern was to control the delivery and prevent the child from coming too fast. The baby was indeed small, but it cried immediately. The first cry is a huge relief for everyone. It is a thrill to the mother and the father. Few realize how great a miracle that cry is. The baby will be all right.

At that moment the bedroom door opened so that the grandparents could see the new baby. Through that open door bounded the sheep dog, who had been patiently awaiting his grand moment of entrance. The dog jumped on the bed. The mother wrapped her arms around the dog's neck and said, "Oh Shep, how nice of you to come to see the baby!"

Eileen said, "Oh my God!"

What I said should not be repeated here.

Phyllis's baby was premature. It had to go to the hospital. Mother and grandmother did not understand this and refused the transfer. The baby would not nurse.

Mother could not be expected to have milk for another one or two days. The baby must be fed and kept warm. A baby that will not nurse, suck or eat will lose weight and weaken to the place that it will die. Over a period of three days the baby did lose weight and become lethargic. I knew that the child must be taken from the home and trusted to the care of nurses trained in this task. We took the baby to the hospital. The mother cried.

It was a good baby. Nurses at the hospital knew what to do. In a week the baby was home and has grown up to be an outstanding person.

The mother remembers only that I took her baby away from her.

I'm sorry. What I remember is the dog!

* * *

Sometimes babies come too fast. Prospective fathers are bewildered by the complexities of the female reproductive process. There is no reason why they should be obstetrically competent. They tend to let their wives be alone at the most critical part of their pregnancies. Bob was the music teacher at the high school. Beth's "due date" was on Friday—three days away. They lived in a small house six miles up the Chewach River north of Winthrop. On Tuesday, Beth was alone. She realized that the day for a new baby was here—right now! A telephone call could not find her husband. Her next call was to us at the medical center—fifteen miles to the south. A doctor can tell by how a woman talks that she is in a labor that will not wait for a routine trip to hospital. My nurse Eileen and I were in my car, along with our birthing equipment, in about three minutes.

When we arrived, Beth was on the floor in the final stages of delivery. This is called crowning, and the baby's forehead is forcing its way over the last group of muscles that protect the exit from the vaginal canal. With one sweep of her arm, Eileen cleared the dining room table of all of the breakfast dishes. There was a crash as the debris hit the floor. Milk spilled and coffee splashed. Eileen then grasped Beth by the right arm and knee while I did the same on the left side. We lifted her to the table. Two chairs appeared and were properly situated for support of the mother's legs (Eileen had done this before). With little effort we assisted a new baby boy into the world on a table splattered with bacon grease and pancake syrup.

Shortly thereafter, the father arrived. By then Eileen had cleaned the kitchen floor and was re-setting the table while I moved the mother into a bedroom.

The father was grateful for our help. He congratulated Beth on how easy it was to have a baby and how nice and natural the birthing process is. This was my first experience with an out-of-hospital delivery. It really is easy when there are no complications.

Chapter 17

Reflections

IN SOLO RURAL PRACTICE OF MEDICINE, your life is always out of balance. Even as a flight surgeon in the U.S. Navy, there were definite times when you were at home and there were definite times when you were at work. Your life tended to be predictable. You had the night duty one day in every four. At those times you stayed at the station hospital at night. Your wife could count on your being at home most other nights.

There were occasional exceptions. As a flight surgeon you were on thirty-minute standby at all times to accompany the Coast Guard on a medically significant rescue. Sometimes these missions took you away from home for several days. They were almost always filled with challenge, danger, unpredictability—and satisfactions.

When I went into private solo practice of family medicine in a rural town in Washington, the rhythm of my life became unpredictable. I was a father, husband, repairman around the house, and family picnic director. But it soon became apparent that I had built a jealous mistress into my life. That jealous mistress was the way I made a living.

Soon my wife became aware that my commitment to my patients tended to come first. I found that if I did not respond to my patients' needs and demands, they would go elsewhere. The doctors in nearby communities had their own jealous mistresses and they, too, responded to their demands. It was a situation that I had not encountered in my training nor in the Navy.

I couldn't plan to do anything with my family without the fear of an interruption. Those interruptions came at any time of the day or night. Since I was in solo practice, I had to respond—often at great inconvenience to myself and my family. I postponed vacations. I left social affairs and dinners because someone had something in his or her eye. I remember leaving a social dinner for the doctors of the county. A mother had called to say that her son had a fever and was twitching. Instead of calling the hospital, the mother called me. I went. Her son did have a fever. He was not convulsing. I remember this case so well because it was the last case of measles that I have seen. It was 1965.

After I reassured the mother and tended to her son's fever, I drove back to the dinner, a round-trip distance of seventy miles. My colleagues from around the county smiled and made comments about the change in lifestyle I was undergoing. They were doing the same thing, to some degree—but all of them had associates or partners. They still had the luxury of a duty schedule that put some balance in their lives.

I don't know if it was good or bad for me to have stayed. But I liked what I was doing, and I thought there would be time for my family later. How many people make that mistake!

It was certainly good for the residents of the Methow Valley. They were beginning to like me and to develop some trust in my judgment. But my personal life was interrupted at all hours and all days of the week. The interruptions came without regard for my personal activities, and sometimes those activities were very personal. I continually congratulated myself on my loyalty to my patients. My wife had a far different opinion.

I was developing a great deal of medical versatility. I took great pride in the fact that I was doing complex surgery. I did my own cesarean sections and operative obstetrics. I waded a bit into the waters of psychiatry. I found the waters too deep and withdrew. My training was strictly Freudian, and by 1970 that skill was obsolete. It was great basic science, but in a busy solo rural practice it had little therapeutic value. In addition, I found that insurance companies and the patients themselves were reticent to pay the doctor for just sitting there, talking and listening.

Because the nearest hospital was forty miles away, I did complex things in my office. I found that I could see patients in their homes for follow-up care much more conveniently than traveling eighty miles round trip to the hospital. I even started doing obstetrics in my office emergency room. One near-tragedy changed all of that, and everyone now goes to the hospital if there is time.

I talk much of the Twisp Medical Center which I built at great expense in 1967. Before that year I practiced in a small office next door to one of the town's better watering holes. I did it all in seven hundred square feet. My personal office was in the hallway, which made it difficult to move wheelchairs from room to room. The rent was seventy-five dollars a month.

When I opened Twisp Medical Center on 5.5 acres of land at the edge of town seven years later, there were many changes. I was locked into a $100,000 mortgage, which extracted $613 a month from an already thin budget. But I was helped by the fact that the economy of the Methow Valley had gradually changed from a barter system to a money economy. I was asked less often if it would be acceptable to pay my bill in hay or fence posts or pack trips or sides of beef. The medical center not only paid for itself, but the mortgage was actually paid off in fewer than the predicted twenty years.

I now had a 3200 square foot building, a large parking lot, and five acres of grass to care for. (The five acres provided the heliport that was used more and more often in emergencies.)

Expenses expanded. I changed my own sprinklers to irrigate the grass (we live in a very dry climate). I mowed the five acres myself. I shoveled the snow from the flat-roofed carport that protected my ambulances. My presence around the Henry homestead was becoming less and less.

Yet, I stayed. My family grew up. The house and the medical center were paid for. The kids were educated and were starting families of their own. Ann earned her master's degree and went to work for a local community college.

I listed the medical center for sale. It did not sell. It was listed for sale for several years without an inquiry. Somehow, doctors were no longer interested in being solo rural family doctors. I worked on. I sometimes wondered whether the medical center was an anchor, dragging me down, rather than a monument to my success. I wondered whether my own idealism and my parents' idealism had played a dirty trick on me by encouraging this lifestyle. I became depressed. Then, in the midst of my depression, there entered Miriam Williams.

On a Sunday afternoon I was relaxing at home with my family and grandchildren. I received a call for an ambulance to respond to a vehicle crash a few miles south of my home. It was urgent. A car was upside down with the occupant trapped inside. My son-in-law and I got the ambulance. We sped to the crash scene. A station wagon had rolled over and the tailgate had been thrown open. I entered the car from the back. I was able to get the woman out of the driver's seat onto a special stretcher that we had developed. With the help of some bystanders, we extricated her from the car and carried her to the ambulance.

While I was making her safe for the trip to the medical center, the gasoline dripping from the carburetor of her car caught fire and burned the front of the wrecked vehicle. I hardly noticed because of the extreme extent of her injuries. With my son-in-law driving, I called on the radio for medical help. The emergency technicians and nurses were waiting at the medical center when we arrived. We had to put a tube in her airway to enable her to breathe. One of the nurses started intravenous infusions into two veins in her arms. She had suffered profound blood loss. The intravenous solutions ran wide open. We then wrapped her in a set of MAST trousers. This is an externally applied G-suit that supports the circulation below the waist. It also had the ability to stabilize her pelvic fracture.

We were then faced with an urgent ambulance trip

of one hundred miles so she could have the care of several medical specialists. I called out my most cautious driver, who had never been known to run a stop sign or a red light. He drove within the speed limit at all times. This time I told him to pull out all of the stops and see what that ambulance would do on the straight-away. We made it and with a bit of time to spare.

The trip was so out of character for this driver that I had to drive him home. The patient was alive and survived the emergency surgeries to which she was subjected. To get her lungs functioning again required more than a month of respiratory therapy. She was eighteen years old.

When she was discharged from that hospital, she traveled to her home in Oregon. Two years later I received an invitation to her wedding. It was accompanied by a personal note thanking me for what I had done. She could not remember the details but she said that in my absence she would have died. She was correct.

I kept that invitation and her picture that she sent me. So, you see why I stayed.

Eventually I did sell the medical center. Then I worked for a medical school at the University of North Dakota, helping direct a training program in family medicine. I worked as a temporary doctor for communities with no physician. I worked a cruise ship as ship's doctor for a trip from Los Angeles to Alaska.

I am now comfortably retired, full of good memories and bad memories. The good lead the bad by a ratio of eighty to twenty. If another opportunity to practice mountain medicine or wilderness medicine arises in the next few years, I'll be tempted to accept the challenge.

You see, I know that I will live forever.

DR. WILLIAM J. HENRY was born in Jeannette, Pennsylvania, in 1929. He attended South Hills High School in Pittsburgh and Grove City College in Grove City, Pennsylvania. After medical school at the University of Pittsburgh, he joined the Navy and served for five years. He settled in Twisp, Washington, after marrying Ann Dwinelle in Jamestown, New York, in 1953. They brought five children into this world: Susan (Cusick), Cindy (Button), Laura (Grimstad), Jane (now deceased), and Bill (Henry). Ten grandchildren are now included in the family album.

Order Form

To order additional copies of *Pay You in Hay*, please fill
out the form below and send to:

ANN HENRY
987 TWISP CARLTON RD.
TWISP, WA 98856

All proceeds go to Aero Methow Rescue Service

- -

Name _____

Address _____

City _____ State _____ Zip _____

Phone (____) _____

Please send me ____ copies of
Pay You in Hay at $10.00 per copy.

_____ x $10.00 = _____
quantity   subtotal

plus shipping & handling = _____
$2.00 (for 1-2 books) $2.50 (for 3-5 books)
$3.00 (for 6-7 books) $3.50 (for 8-10 books)   shipping & handling

_____
TOTAL ENCLOSED